NOT ONE WORLD

Martin McGeown

Cover by Rachael Darley

ISBN: 9798760558589

First Edition

Disclaimer:
Unless otherwise indicated, all the names, characters, businesses, places, events, and incidents in this book are either the product of the author's imagination or used in a fictitious manner. Any resemblance to actual persons, living or dead, or actual events is purely coincidental.

CONTENTS

ACKNOWLEDGMENTS

Overwhelming thanks to Rachael Darley, for the complete design of the book cover. She managed to accomplish the eye grabbing appearance and also contain features of the story itself, overall creating a piece fitting for a fantasy fiction such as this.

And my infinite gratitude will forever go out to Paul Perry, for his much appreciated work in actually getting the book to where it is now. I never could have done it without his help in editing end publishing. Paul helped me achieve my dream.

DEDICATION

My amazing Mother and Father

Loving little brother

Saint of a Grandmother

Abigail Perry

Amelia Quinn

Aoibhinn Taylor

Aoife Berry

Gabriela Martinez Angulo

Cai Ashby

Clodagh Deweer

Diana Marcova

Aisling Durnin

Kate Champion

Katie Char

Jane Wilson Burke

THE VERY BEGINNING

~~~

The Garden surrounded by flowers really is the best place to sit and ponder. Gather one's thoughts. Magic was the very life force of these exotic blooms. That is why they are so magnificent. There is one that grows fruit that tastes like the thing you desire the most. There is also one that releases a mist that if you smell it, it makes you light as air itself. This place was special to me. I remember having picnics with my dear mother. I remember watching the passing ships fly by and my friends and I would spot as many white ones as we could. I remember my father showing me what the magic inside me could do. Spending hours giving up and him always convincing me to go at it again. That is the world I live in. Sorry, I need to do some explaining, don't I? Well, let's start at the beginning…the VERY beginning……

A tremendous explosion in the middle of complete nothingness. Life being scattered for trillions of miles. Like dropping a bag of marbles on the floor and watching them go all over the place. Everything went everywhere. Stars, planets, and galaxies were
~~~

created within a blink of an eye. This is what the residents of earth call the Big Bang. I even believe they made a Television production on it. Anyway, this was the beginning of life itself. The creation of the very Universe everything exists in. But the Bang didn't create everything…The Legend states the explosion ripped the fabric of space and time and the tear gave life to something of its own. The first and most powerful being in all existence. Zeus, King of the gods. He didn't know why he was there, and he didn't know how. But what he did know was that our Universe wasn't big enough in his eyes. So, using his unfathomable abilities, he went back through the tear in space he came from and created many other worlds, dimensions, realms filled with magical creatures, objects, and people. The life of magic and worlds beyond normality that most people are familiar with, began. He created Gods to watch over his worlds and they built civilizations within those realms. Many realms sprung to life and trillions of magical people live in prosperity in realms of magic. Sadly, after millions of years Zeus using his extraordinary powers, his body gave up on him, so he laid himself to rest in a distant realm that no one has any knowledge of. Not even the Gods he gave life to. The Universe was without a king for the first time since its creation.

Of course, people can't always keep the peace so of course there have been wars. My father Triton

Griffin is the God of revenge and he was a warlord maniac determined to conquer all he could. Now he's not as bad as he sounds. Yes, he was the most ruthless God in 16 realms, but he had a change of heart, literally. He wished to conquer my mother Rhea's realm, so he and his army invaded without mercy. My mother sent out her forces because she wasn't going to go down without a fight. After an epic battle between the two armies it seemed they were at an impasse, neither one could conquer the other. But my mother was the Goddess of Love. She had the sacred ability to reform evil hearts if there was love and passion between the cursed heart and another. So, when she and my father met each other's gaze, it was love at first sight and Triton's heart was filled with light and good. His evil ways were no more. The wars between him and the other realms were over, that little bit more piece to the universe was restored.

They decided to start their own realm together. Wanting a fresh start and place they could call theirs. They ventured across the universe together, searching for the perfect place to start their own realm. They had many encounters during their adventures but the best one was when they discovered what I now call home. Atlasdam, a beautiful and remote place with exotic magical creatures, waterfalls, and blue skies. They knew it when they first laid eyes on it that it was the place. The place that a new civilization would start. They invited many people to help build in exchange for a place to call home. Of course, like every city it started out small. But after a few thousand years, it grew and grew and it wasn't so small anymore. It became one of the greatest cities across the realms and came to be the realm of peace. Our people, the Atlians, adored their leaders and showered them with much appreciation. My parents got married and the city then had a royal family who adored their subjects as much as the son they had soon after their marriage.

My name is Raven Griffin, son of Triton and Rhea Griffin. The prince of Atlasdam, and this is my story.

I was extremely happy with my family. I had many picnics with my mother in the gardens I mentioned earlier. My father would take me flying in his old airship and try to show me how to use the power that was passed down to me. When I say 'try' I mean he would show me and I would fail to do so. I remember when me and my friends would spend our days counting the different colors of the different airships passing by. I was happy. But on one fateful day, all that I loved and knew was taken away from me...

My mother and father were on their morning walk and they came across a strange grey bush. It was covered in green fruit and looked as though it had the life drained from it. Rhea went to take a closer look but suddenly a giant black serpent jumped out of the bush and sickened its long venomous fangs into my mother's ankle. My father destroyed the snake in seconds, but not before the venom corrupted my dear mother.

She began to transform. Her skin turned to scales. She grew razor sharp talons. Her hair fell out and a dozen snakes rose in its place. She transformed into a monster, a being of malice and hatred. They called her Medusa, the goddess of darkness. She rampaged the city, turning people to stone with a single glare. As everyone ran and screamed, I was in the gardens playing with my friends, not knowing what had just occurred. But then I saw the beast. The thought that it could have been my mother never set foot into my head. My mother was sweet. My mother was kind. This monster was evil incarnate. She saw me and charged. I attempted to run but her claws were too quick for my small child's legs. She held me in front of her wicked eyes and somehow, I saw my mother in those red rubies that sat in her corrupted head. But she didn’t turn me to stone, instead she laughed at my despair and stomped her foot and the ground began to quake. The earth opened up and Medusa with me in her clutches, slid into the earth. She dragged me kicking and screaming into the depths of the underworld, never to be seen again…

2

THE GREAT ESCAPE

~~~

Medusa dragged me down, down deep into the fiery depths of the underworld. I tried to the best of my ability to escape but it was no use. She was far too strong for my puny child strength. I felt myself getting warmer and my messy brown hair started getting wet with my perspiration. We kept going down and down until we arrived at a cave that was the housing of a whole other realm. It was like a kingdom down there. I saw this evil looking fortress perched over the lava sea where ships made of a fireproof material sailed. The fortress was made of a crimson red brick and had guards surrounding every square inch of it. This was a truly evil realm. We reached the underworld floor and Medusa dropped me on the hot floor. I stood up and tried to run, but that was easier said than done. I felt as though my body was being dragged down by an invisible force. The heat was immensely overbearing and my body got heavier and heavier until I collapsed and blacked out.
~~~

It was complete blackness. The muffled sound of chains rattling echoed in my ears. There was a voice but I didn't know what they were saying. I opened my eyes and sat up. As they started to focus, I could make out a small red figure stomping towards me.

"Didn't you ear' me?! I said ge' to work!" shouted the little red man.

With my eyes fully focused at this point I could get a good look at exactly what was talking to me. He was a small red little goblin at elbow height with jagged teeth and beady eyes. His long red ears drooped down to where his neck was supposed to be and he had stubby little legs.

"Grow spine ye useless git! Grab a pickaxe and get to work!" He shouted in my face and sprayed spit everywhere.

I got to my feet and grabbed a pickaxe. "Now yer' digging for this". He reached into a small pocket of his and plucked out a little gemstone. I moved closer to inspect it, between his two fingers was a red crystal with black specks dotted around it.

"Is that a ruby?" I asked.

"No, you idiot! It's called Demonite, Medusa needs it for her army. So, if I wer' you I would ge' to swinging!" He yelled once more, stormed off and began shouting at someone else.

I got to my feet and tried to move but didn't. I tried to move again but my body was pulled back. Not knowing what was going on, I looked down and saw that my leg was attached to a ball and chain. It was cruel, but not as cruel as what I saw next. Around me were hundreds of other people swinging pickaxes at the cave walls. They were slaves, innocent people all in chains and forced to work their life away. Some looked like they have been there for many years, starved and weak. Well, that's what happened to me. For years I slaved away in those mines and no one came for me. Ten long grueling years went by and I was still swinging that pickaxe aimlessly. Ten long years of suffering and cruelty.

After a rough day of mining, I was in my cell curled up in a ball sobbing on the floor like every other night in the corner of the room. Being alone, with no love, no kindness of any sort really did its worst on me. I wanted to feel the warm embrace of my parents again. To feel their arms around me once more, or even a chance to properly say goodbye. Maybe there was still good in my mother? If only I could see her again. For the years I spent down in those mines suffering, I never saw her once. But then it hit me. Magic ran through my blood. I could use it to break out of here. I hadn't been trained to use them, but it was all I had. I was sixteen now so maybe they were strong enough.

The Guard was coming round with the gruel they called food and I pretended to sob again.

"Eat up spineless" he said and threw it through the bars onto the floor, splatting it everywhere.

When he turned around, I saw the rusted sparkle of the keys attached to his waist. I snuck up behind him and tried to grab them through the bars but he walked away too fast. But with my hand reached out, I closed my eyes and imagined the keys coming to my hand. Picturing it vividly in my mind, I concentrated and felt the determination flowing through me. I opened my eyes and the keys were aglow with a red light, floating towards me. Next thing I knew they were in my hand. I always knew deep down I had it in me.

I waited for it to get late even though I had no concept of what time of day it was, since I was a million miles underground and could not see the sky. All the guards had fallen asleep so that's when I decided to make my move. I quietly turned the key until I heard the click and gently pushed the cell door. But my blood ran cold when it made a really loud creak and I thought my cover was blown. I froze and waited to be swarmed by guards. Luckily the coast was clear and my nerves calmed down. I snuck out of the cell lock without a trace and tried to figure a way out of this ghastly place. Wandering the fortress halls for ages was pointless when I realized it was hardly going to be possible for a sixteen-year-old, barely able to use his powers to escape a realm that was millions of miles under the surface.

I wanted to return to my cell and continue my suffering rather than risk facing the wrath of the guards. Suddenly I heard voices. Riskily peeking my head round the corner, the fear set in my skull when I saw that I was looking directly into the throne room, and on the throne, was Medusa herself. The room itself screamed evil. There were crimson flame torches dotted around and there were cages hanging from the ceiling. But what was in the cages scared me the most. Bodies. Lifeless, fleshless bodies. This immoral monster was captivating innocent souls and leaving them to fade away. I swore to Zeus himself that if I make it out of here alive and manage to get back home then I would free every last one of these slaves and shut down this operation forever. There was a red goblin standing next to the throne and he looked just as scared as I was. I tried to listen to what they were talking about.

"But my lady, we still have many to go and-"

There was a loud thump, Medusa stomped her foot in anger. "I don't care what it takes! The ritual can't commence without all of them! Every last one!!!"

The goblin swallowed the apple in his throat and built up what little courage he had and spoke again.

"We have all our spies out as we speak, but nearly every realm is heavily guarded ever since you kidnapped your son. Triton must have-"

There was a louder thump. "DON'T RELATE THAT WEAK LITTLE FOOL TO ME!" Medusa Bellowed as it echoed throughout the underworld. My heart sank, deep down I thought there was a part of my mother left, but it turns out I was greatly mistaken. My mother Rhea was well and truly gone, that snake corrupted every inch of her pure heart.

"I'm sorry my queen, but without an army we can't invade the realms".

Medusa clenched her fist in frustration. She couldn't believe she was talking to such an imbecile. "You fool, once our master continues their plan, the universe will bow down to us. One by one, they all will fall like perfectly placed dominoes." She laughed her evil laugh and it echoed once again, creating even more mental scares in my mind.

That laugh still haunts me to this day. Hearing the hatred filled laugh in mind stopped me from realizing I had to get out of here. Opposite me was a stairwell that led up, but there was one problem. I had to cross the entrance of the throne room to get to it. And if I did cross, I would be in full eyeshot of Medusa. I quickly tried to think and hit my head in frustration, but when I looked up to see what I hit my head on, I saw a chandelier hanging down.

The chain I hit my head on was on the wall too. That's when I had the awful idea. I shimmied up the chain and made it to a thin ledge up high. The chandelier was directly in front of me. Now before I tell you what I did next, I just wanted to say I was very desperate to escape and this was the only idea I had. I leaped from the ledge, grabbed the chandelier, and pulled myself up. I actually made it, but my luck ran out. The chain bolted to the ceiling gave away and the chandelier came crashing down bringing me along with it.

Medusa's head shot at the loud crash and saw the collapsed pile of metal, then she saw me emerge from the dust.

"HE'S ESCAPED! STOP HIM!"

I dashed up the stairwell with the monster right behind me crashing into every wall and step with her large body.

"GET BACK HERE BOY!" she shrieked and I went even faster.

The fear drove me to climb and stumble for dear life but I had finally reached the top and got a blast of immense heat. My bloodshot eyes darted in every direction, looking for something evil right on my tail. Without a thought I used my magic to pick up a giant ball I found and hurled it at the archway over the stairwell. It turns out that ball was an explosive and the archway collapsed, blocking Medusa, or at least slowing her down. I heard a thud on the other side of the rubble followed by repeated pounding and shouting. I continued to run but I didn't know where to go. How was I meant to escape? I dove behind a crate to catch my breath and go over my options considering I didn't have many. I was wiping the sweat from my face when I heard more voices. I peeked behind the crate and saw more goblins standing beside an airship.

"Shipment of Demonite from the northern mines." Bellowed the goblin coming off the ship.

They started unloading the crates off the ship and that's when another crazy idea popped into my head. While their backs were turned, I snuck onto the deck of the ship and grabbed the helm. I pulled the long lever beside the helm towards me and the airship jolted into action.

"Wait we're missing a cra-, WAIT HOLD ON GET BACK HERE!". The goblins noticed me and I panicked.

My hand gripped the handle firmly and pulled the lever even further and the ship propelled forward. Trying to control the hastily moving aircraft was harder than it looked and I had no idea what I was doing. There was a red button on a panel, I pushed it and the ship suddenly came to a stop propelling me into the wheel, so obviously that was the button for the brakes.

As I tried to gather myself, I heard a very loud thump, followed by a big crash. It was Medusa finally getting through that wall, and boy was she mad. She saw me on the airship and stared into my soul. She yelled in extreme anger. She clenched her fists and looked as though she was channeling her powers. But then she started to grow. She grew and grew until she hit her head off the underworld ceiling. She was a titanic size and even towered over the fortress. She roared and the entire realm quaked at the sound of it. I had never been more scared in my life. My trembling arm grabbed the lever and heaved it towards me and the ship accelerated. Medusa's strides were giant and she was constantly right behind me. She swung her colossal hand and the ship was in her grasp. She held onto a cliff and pulled me and the ship back. I pulled the lever as far as it would go but it wasn't enough for Medusa's strength. My fear overcame me and tears rolled down my face. I was scared and didn't know what to do. I was between a rock and a hard place.

Rock...I thought. Trying to see behind the titan, I looked up and there was a large stalagmite coming downright above Medusa. So, I had the idea to make it collapse onto her to make her let go. I held my hand out and channeled the little strength I had left into my palms and released it into a surge of energy. A Shining ball of red energy escaped my palms and struck the dripping stone. The stalagmite cracked and gave away, coming down on top of the monster, but she didn't do anything except grunt, it didn't do anything. I had no energy left, what was I going to do? But suddenly I heard more cracking. Medusa froze and glared at me. The whole ceiling caved and came crashing down on top of Medusa. Hundreds of stalagmites fell from the cave ceiling and pierced her scaly flesh, taking her life.

The ship launched in incredible speed as she let go. I cried as I looked back at my evil mother's lifeless body. Even though she kidnapped me and put me through hell, I still wished to hug her once more. The ship kept picking up speed going faster and faster until......POOF. The ship along with me vanished into the humid underworld air. I was gone.......

3

A NEW WORLD

~~~

Peace and quiet on still chilly night. Not a thing moving besides the tall grass in the gentle breeze. All that ended when I came falling from the sky on a broken airship. The ship was hurling towards the ground and my weak arms held on to dear life as the rest of my body furled in the air. The ground was getting very close very fast. I quickly made a magic shield around me to protect me, then the ship plummeted to the ground, knocking me out.

Eventually I came around and I was surrounded by debris. I wasn't hurt so my shield must have worked but I had a splitting headache. I sat up still a bit dizzy and looked around. The ship landed in a field of tall grass and it made a long crater in it. I got to my feet and searched the wreckage for anything useful. Besides from an old map and a broken pickaxe, I came up empty handed. Not really knowing what to do from there, I began following the long crater the ship made. It went on for quite a while but eventually I made it to the end. At the
~~~

end I found a road that seemed to go on longer than the crater did. As I looked down the road, I saw a small light that gradually got brighter until I could see the light was emanating from something. A small Vehicle rolled up the road. It had four wheels, two lights and a cockpit. The window on it slowly came down and the man inside peeked his head out.

"You alright son?" he asked and looked me up and down.

Just so you know I was in an awful state. My clothes were ripped to shreds and hanging off me. There was a streak of dry blood on my face and I was thoroughly covered head to toe in dirt. The man looked dead straight into my red eyes and a slight form of confusion appeared on his face. After I realized this, I spoke up.

"Uh yeah, excuse me but what realm is this?" I asked, trying to look as normal as possible.

The man looked at me as if I was a crazy person. "Look kid I'll give you a ride to town but that's as far as I'm going.......freak." he said under his breath.

I hopped in with the man and we drove down the road. I tried many times to start a conversation with him but I was very unsuccessful. Every response was either 'yeah' or 'mhm', so we stayed silent for the duration of the journey. Without saying a word, he reached into a little compartment in front of him and pulled out a little cloth.

He handed it to me and said, "for your face". I looked at him but he didn't look back, his eyes still dead straight on the road.

"Thank you" I said and wiped the blood on my face.

As we kept driving, we started approaching a small town by a beach, but it was nothing like any town I have seen. Most of the buildings were small and mostly made of brick and glass. There was no palace or flying ships. But there was one aircraft, but it had wings and engines where our ships fly with magic.

"Welcome to Hampton Beach, kid." the man said as the vehicle came to a stop. I got out, he wished me luck and disappeared into the night.

The night brought a chill as I had barely any clothes. I wandered the streets looking for somewhere to sleep. The few people that were out just looked at me weirdly and kept on walking, not one of them offered me help. In Atlasdam, help was always given to those who needed It. Obviously it was vastly different in this world. I continued to wander like a lost soul but then I came across a curious little building. It had a symbol of a book on the door and said 'open'. It must have been a library. I walked in and I was surrounded by warmth and the feeling of relaxation.

“Can I help you?” said a voice from behind me. I turned around and it was a pale old woman. She was short and scrawny and wore glasses that sat at the end of her nose. She looked at me with a twinkle in her eyes and a smile on her face. There was something awfully familiar about her, as if she had been a part of my whole life. She had this atmosphere about her that felt kind and gentle and you couldn’t help wanting to be around her.

“Uh hello...” I said awkwardly.

“Was there something you needed dear?” she asked sweetly.

“No, I'm okay, I was just going to take a look around. Is that alright?”

She chuckled “Of course dear, no knowledge here is forbidden”. She walked away and disappeared behind a bookcase.

I began scanning the spines of the books, looking for something on the culture of this world. I ended up settling on a book with a blue ball on the front with green patches on it and read ‘Planet Earth for dummies’. I sat down at a table and began reading. I read about the culture of ‘Planet Earth’ and what people do. Many people have jobs in Atlasdam like Apothecary or Sorceress but on earth there's jobs like accountants and lawyers which I had never heard of. There was also something called the President of the United States which kind of sounded like a king. I read what the kids did. They went to a local school and 'hung out' at other people's homes. Home...it made me think of mine. The only family and place I ever loved, taken away from me. Forced to kill my own mother corrupted by darkness. My father probably worried sick. What did he think was happening to me? Putting every ounce of his energy searching every inch of every realm for me.

I put my face in my hands and cried my eyes out. I knew I would never see my family again. It's been ten years and my father would have assumed I was dead. I was whimpering now, my face and hands wet with tears. As I continued to sob pathetically, I felt a slight poking at my leg. It was the librarian. She looked up at my puffy red face with those friendly eyes.

"Come with me" she said and slowly walked away. I wiped my face and watched her walk away, slightly confused but then I soon followed her.

She led me into a quiet room behind a curtain. The room was decorated to truly fit the mood of relaxation. The dim candles, the sage burning and the soothing ambiance playing softly.

"Sit" she said and pointed to a cushion in front of

her.

I sat down and crossed my legs. The woman poured a warm liquid into a cup and handed it to me.

"Tranquil tea calms the nerves and clears the mind". She took a sip and her shoulders eased up and she closed her eyes.

I brought the cup to my mouth and let the tea pass my lips. As it entered my system, a warm feeling overcame me. The warmth spread all the way to my fingertips and reached the back of my head. I thought of all the happy things even though I was in a rough place. My blood came to a slow flow and I was able to feel safe in my own skin for once in ten years.

"Tell me child, what has you in such distress?" she asked.

This complete stranger was willing to hear my story. A woman who has no idea what I've encountered and experienced was ready to drop everything and listen to a poor grieving boy. Then again, she didn't look like she had much going on. My eyes met hers and the light glistened in her glasses.

"My family, my home, taken away from me." I whispered in sadness, swallowing the large lump in my throat.

She gazed at me as if she was reading my soul. The cup was perched at her lips as she took another sip of her tea and spoke.

"I may be just an old lady, but I have had my own happenings and experiences. I too lost my family, but the past is something we cannot change, but the future is what we make it."

The last drop of tea slid down my throat as these words ran around my mind. As sad as I was and as much as I wanted to see my family, this old woman was right. There was nothing I could do, I had to look forward, but I had nowhere to go.

"Where can I go? I lost everything I held dear. I have no home".

She put the cup down beside her and stood up. She walked over to a shelf in the corner of the room and came back with a little wooden box.

"I would let you stay here, but that star in your eyes says you want some place to call your own". I smiled at her and nodded. "Well, I want to give this to you". Her gentle hands opened the box and plucked out a small silver key. She placed it in my hand and closed it with hers.

"Why are you being so nice to me? You don't even know me". Not that I didn't appreciate it, I was simply confused.

"Help should always be given to those who need it. You don't need to be a detective to see that".

A tear formed in my eye, I felt loved. "Thank you" I whispered, "But who are you?" I needed to know the name of this wonderful woman.

"Charissa dear". I held her hand tightly.

"Thank you Charissa, my name is Raven. You have my eternal gratitude".

"Go" she said "Change your future"

4

HOME AWAY FROM HOME

~~~

Wrapped in the warm coat Charissa gave me, I followed the directions she had written on a piece of paper. I didn't know what was at the end of the rainbow but I was excited to find out. I came across a street with a line of houses on each side. The paper said to go straight down and my destination was the end. So, I followed the tall lights down the dark street. It was very eerie, not a single soul was about. The cold between my toes was starting to sting but I kept walking, but suddenly I heard a loud crash that scared the living daylights out of me. My head spun to where it came from and it was a stupid cat in a metal canister. It hissed at me and scurried up the street. As I kept walking, I could make out the shape of a small building in front of the moonlight. It was a house, and it was where the directions were leading me. I walked up the gravel path and tripped many times as it was very dark. When I reached the front door, I took out the special key Charissa gave me and put it in the door. It twisted until I heard the click and I stepped
~~~

inside.

The house was cold and pitch black. There were no candles or anything. If there was a candle, I could have used it to guide me to a bed until the morning. Then I thought, if I could kill a fifty-foot monster, I could make a little light with my magic. With my hand held out, I channeled power into my fingertips. I imagined the room aglow and then my hand sparked. There was a small ball of light floating in my hands. I don't want to gloat but it was beautiful to look at. It wasn't extremely bright but it was enough to see where I was going. As I walked around the house, I kept sneezing because of the big clouds of dust. I walked into several cobwebs and got my foot stuck in a floorboard. This place was really a fixer upper, but it was all I had, so I had to work with what I got. Eventually, I found my way to a bedroom and tried to settle down for the night, but that was easier said than done. I had to find my way to a bed in the dark room. I stubbed many toes and tripped on a rug. When the bed was finally in my reach, it was all worn and torn and littered with dust. I patted it down and a dark dust cloud arose from it. I ripped the bed clothes off and waved it in the air to make it somewhat clean, but when I took everything off the bed, it revealed a spring sticking out of the mattress. Could this night get any worse? I decided to lie on the other side and wrap up warm. With my jacket still on, I threw the duvet around me and laid my head on the pillow, inhaling more dust and coughing it back up again. I eventually fell asleep and waited for the morning to come

It was complete blackness once again. Gazing into the familiar sight that was nothingness. I could hear a faint sound. It sounded familiar, as if I grew up with it. My eyes slowly opened and the sound became clear. I was home in Atlasdam. The city was cheering for my safe return. My father in the middle of it, his arms wide open ready to welcome his son back into his life. I ran towards him, tears running down face, my mind racing at a hundred miles, but I stopped dead in my tracks when I blinked. The city was burning; the cheering was replaced by painful screaming. Everyone was suffering, the city was destroyed and my father's severed head in Medusa's hand.

I woke up in an awful panic, my breathing out of control. Sweat was dripping from my face and arm pits. My heart was beating rapidly, feeling it against my hand as I held my chest. It was only a dream, a really intense realistic dream. The dust was sticking to my sweaty face and I was in direct shot of the sunlight peeping through the curtains. Now that there was light, I could finally see the house in all its broken glory. The room I slept in had furniture covered in white sheets and the walls were a lovely crème color with a brown wooden strip along the upper wall. I tried to think about something besides the dream, hoping that's all it was, a dream and not some vision of the future. I got up out of that filthy bed and began ripping the white sheets off the furniture. There was a tall wardrobe, a dresser, and a bedside locker, all having this unique nature like design carved into them. The room was extremely humid so I threw the windows open and let the fresh air in. I sat on the windowsill and embraced the quiet and peaceful atmosphere. The fresh ocean air was really beneficial. Ten years of that foul underworld air really took its toll on my lungs. The view from the window was astonishing. The crystal-clear blue waters reminded me of home. My mother had this small boat and we would go float on the lake's shallow waters. I would always purposely fall in and splash Rhea. Then I would end up dragging her in with me and we would both trek home soaking wet. We would then warm up by the fire while my father regaled us with his great adventures across the universe. I remembered how well he described his encounters; it was almost like I was there with him. I would have really likened his help; we could have fixed up this house together.

He told me when he was younger, he fixed many first-place airship racers and also fixed many evil battleships for warlords. He was ashamed every single time he told me those stories. But the only thing that mattered was that he changed. He may have harmed many innocent beings, but he helped even more in the long run.

As emotional as I was getting, I remembered Charissa's words.

"The past is something we cannot change, but the future is what we make it". I knew she was absolutely right, so I had to heed her advice and focus on the task at hand, this house wasn't going to clean itself. So, I rolled up my sleeves and got down to the dirty work.

I began with the room I slept in. It was extremely messy and covered in filth and dust. When I went looking for a sweeping brush, I found a cupboard full of cleaning supplies, some I have seen before, some I have not. A stick covered in feathers was in there as well so I used it to banish the dust and swept the floor until my feet could no longer get dirty. There was a large green container in the front garden where I could dispose of all the rubbish I accumulated over the hours of work I put into cleaning the house. Eventually I had to sit down after the amount of time and effort put into it. For my break I decided to relax and dive deep into a good sample of literature.

I scanned the spines and randomly selected a book but my eyes caught a glimpse of a book behind a small stone statue on the upper shelf. I slid the statue over to grab the book but the bookcase had other ideas. The entire case shook and I fell off the stool I was standing on. I fell to the floor and sat shocked as books nosedived off the shelf. The bookcase stopped shaking and moved to the left and revealed a secret passage. I got to my feet and peered down the dark echoey passage. Without hesitation, I conjured a ball of light and entered the mysterious hall. The hall was cold and musty, no one must have been down here in a long time. I continued down and felt the small presence of cold on my warm nose.

When I made it to the end of the hall, I wandered into this dimly lit room with a single already lit torch. That was most mysterious. How was the torch already lit if no one has been here in ages? I ignored it for the moment and wandered round the room a bit longer but that was once again, easier said than done. I noticed more torches as I looked round the room and lit them as I went. When I lit them all I realized what kind of room I was in. It was a small library with even more books. But the books here weren't like any of the others upstairs. I examined them and every single one of these were books of magic, all of them. Spell books, books on magic relics, magical travel and much more.

Just when I thought this realm was magicless, the circumstances had proved me wrong yet again. I sat confused for a while. Why was this all here? This world was beyond Zeus's creation so there shouldn't be magic. But there was one person that might have known about all this. Charissa was the very person who gave me this house so maybe she knew why this was all here. But what if she didn't? What if I told her and she had no idea what I was talking about and made a fool of myself, let alone expose the Universe of magic to a mere mortal. Also, this could be my chance of getting home. Maybe among all of this mystery was the key to my finally getting back to Atlasdam. I knew I couldn't let this go but I was getting very tired after all my work so I closed up the passageway for now and settled for the night. I would continue digesting my discovery in the morning.

5

NOT ALWAYS AS IT SEEMS

~~~

As much as I wanted to sit down and read every book in that secret room, I had to sort out the current situation I found myself in. I was sixteen now and still hadn't received a substantial education. I regularly went on walks around town to get familiar with the place and I came across what seemed to be a school. The lady at the desk told me to go to their website to get more information. But the problem was I didn't even know what a website was...

I read up on 'Planet Earth for dummies' again and I realized that I had to purchase a 'phone' to go to a website. But my pockets were empty to purchase anything let alone a phone. I just counted myself lucky that Charissa didn't charge me rent. But one day when I went out on my walk, I found a green piece of paper stuck between the wood planks on a bench. On it said twenty dollars and that's when I remembered someone in Charissa's bookshop buying a book with one of these. This must have been this world's currency. Now I couldn't imagine
~~~

being able to buy much with twenty dollars. But I found a spell book in the basement that could change that. The book had all types of spells but the one that I was most interested in was the Duplication spell.

It could duplicate any earthly item. I recited the spell while holding my hand over the note and magically I now had forty dollars. The spell didn't seem to have any limits so I kept using it until I had enough to purchase the phone and also kept some for other things. I went into the phone store and handed the man the required amount to buy the device but he kept asking me questions that I didn't know the answer to.

"Would you like to join our monthly broadband? How about our 15 dollar a month deal?"

I just kept saying no until he let me buy the stupid thing and leave. The device was set up but when I got home to go to a website, I needed something called 'Wi-Fi'. I didn't know what I had to do to purchase that but that's when I remembered I saw a sign outside a restaurant that said, 'Free Wi-Fi'. I went to the restaurant and asked the waiter for the Wi-fi. He told me I need to buy a drink first, so that's what I did. He asked me for my phone and then started tapping it.

"There you go, all set up." he said and handed me back my phone.

A few days had gone by and I had gotten better at using the phone but I still struggled from time to time. I felt like I was six years old again not being able to harness my magic. The lady at the school gave me a long order of letters and I typed them into the web browser. The school's crest popped up and lots of information presented itself. I spent quite a while taking in all the school had to offer and I got overly excited. There was a literature program and a library which interested me the most as I loved to dive into books and get lost. I had already plowed through half the books at my house but I had yet to journey through the magical books in the secret room which I knew I had to do.

I continued scrolling through the website and found out how I could roll into the next term. There was a phone number that I had to dial if I wanted to book a meeting with the principal and have a discussion. My fingers hesitantly tapped each number into my phone and waited. The beeping nose kept going but then I heard a voice.

"Hampton High School's principal, how can I help you?" said the voice. It was a woman and her voice was regal and imposing.

"Um hello" I said, very nervous but bucked up the courage and spoke again." My name is Raven Griffin and I was hoping we could set a time when we could discuss whether I'm qualified to roll into Hampton High". There was a pause and I could hear pages flicking and the sounds of several clicks.

"Well, my name is Rose Noble and I am the principal of our fine establishment. Could you tell me a bit about yourself?" said the principal., "and why can't I speak to your parents?

"Well, um...." I had no idea what to say to this woman. I couldn't just come out and tell her that I was from another world, my mom is dead and my father is a king probably worrying his head off wondering if I'm even alive and that I want to roll into her school because I hadn't received an education in ten years. Making something up was the best option, something believable. "Well, I um... live with my grandmother because my mother and father were......in a terrible car accident...."

"Oh, dear I'm terribly sorry." she interrupted.

"Thank you," I continued. "I'm sixteen years old and have a great interest in reading." I finished.

"Well Raven, thank you for sharing that but is there a way I can maybe speak to your grandmother? I have to speak to a legal guardian If I am to forward this conversation into a meeting."

Another fib popped into my head. "She's actually asleep right now but I would be more than happy to continue this discussion in a meeting myself. My grandmother is hard of hearing so It would be like talking to a revolving door." I covered my mouth as

I giggled but kept my composure as I tried to make a good first impression.

"Right," she said, slightly annoyed. "I suppose we could arrange a date for a meeting but you make sure your grandmother knows that I want to speak with her as soon as possible. Hold on for one moment" she said and there was silence over the phone.

I couldn't believe this was actually working. Finally, I was making progress on my fresh start. I had been waiting ten years for this and it was finally happening. Maybe I could make some new friends. Then I remembered I wouldn't be able to do the things I used to do with my old friends.

My best friends were Ophilia and Alfyn. We did everything together. The inseparable trio. We would spend hours in the gardens, going on our own little 'quests' and sometimes the little stories we made would drag out for days. We would always try to finish our dinner as quickly as possible so we could continue the fun. I remember the passion we felt playing, it was like we were actually fighting against an evil god trying to conquer Atlasdam. Ophilia would always get angry when another twist came into play but Alfyn would never give up until we came out on top. But like all good things, it eventually came to an end. If I made new friends in school then I wouldn't be able to relive those fantastic moments. But as long as I was happy and safe, I guess it didn't matter who I became friends with.

I heard Rose's voice again and there was some background chatter. "Well, Raven I'm afraid I will be terribly busy for the next month but you're welcome to arrive on the first day of term so you can get a feel for our school. It will be a normal school day and I'll set your name into the register".

I listened to her every word very carefully and wrote down what I felt was important. I wasn't going to make a single mistake when it came to my education.

"Thank you so much Mrs. Noble, I won't let you down!"

"I look forward to seeing you in class...." She hung up.

I started dancing down the room with pure joy. I had never been so excited for school. Not only would it help me pursue to change my future like Charissa said. But it would also take my mind off everything that had happened. Then when I thought everything was normal, a sudden feeling came over me. It was a vibration waving through my body and I heard a muffled sound. The sound got clearer and it formed in my mind.

"The legend...........read it.........."

It was a voice. How was I hearing it? What and who was it? I moved around the room to see if the feeling got stronger. The closer I got to the secret passage the voice in my head became clearer.

"The prophecy......"

The eerie voice spun round my mind as I walked down the passage. I felt the feeling in my hands as it radiated to my fingertips. It was close, I could feel it. My voice filled head looked round the room and I held out my hands as if the room was pitch black. With my eyes closed, I followed the feeling inside and my hand came in contact with a book on the case. The lines in the wood glide across my fingertips and when I felt it in a pacific area, I opened my eyes and saw my hand over a book. The feeling was stronger than before. This was it. I slid the book from the self and everything stopped still. The hairs on my neck rested once again.

I stroked the leather of the book and felt the cold of the gold corners on the covers. The book had no title and there was nothing on the front cover. I slowly opened it up and a bright light filled my eyes and another voice entered my mind. This one was a girl; her voice was like a finely tuned instrument as she spoke nobly.

"*A boy of Revenge and Love, will pierce the heart of Malice and vanquish the beckoning Darkness summoned by a mysterious foe.*"

I heard enough and slammed the book closed. I couldn't believe what I had just heard. *A boy of Revenge and love*? That sentence repeated over and over again in my head. It couldn't have been talking about me, could it? I had so many questions, questions that I knew no one in this world could answer. But maybe there was one person....

I ran back up the passage, grabbed my coat and disappeared into the night. My legs ran as fast as they could to find the woman that started it all. I bumped into many people but I didn't care. I needed answers, and I needed them now. I finally arrived at the library but I stopped dead in my tracks. The library was gone.... like it was never there. In its place stood a coffee shop. I swung the door open and my eyes shot around the shop like a rabid animal hunting for its prey. The guy there was cleaning up from a day's business and looked at me as If I had ten heads.

"Where is she..." I whispered, a bead of sweat forming on my forehead.

The guy there had no words.

"WHERE IS CHARISSA!" I shouted at the guy and he stood stoned face.

I realized the situation I now found myself in. I walked out of there dizzy, feeling bad for what I had just done, but that compared to the feeling that sank in my heart.

Where was Charissa? Did she ever exist at all? Was it all a dream?

6

NOT ALONE

~~~

I tossed and turned all night in my bed, afraid to fall asleep and wake from my dream back down in that underworld prison. I could not bear the thought of all that had happened not being real. The escape. Charissa and this amazing house. Was it all real or was it all a dream in the labyrinth I can never seem to escape in my mind? And then there was that thing I found in the basement.

"*A boy of revenge and love, will pierce through the heart of Malice and vanquish the darkness summoned by a mysterious foe*".

I tried to decipher what it meant but my head was all kinds of messed up after the night before. I was too afraid to sleep so I was tired of dragging myself around the house like a zombie, and the worst thing was that I started school the next morning. My nerves were breaking down and my body was shaking with stress. I just sat down and cried like I did every night in the underworld. I knew I had to keep moving forward and stop looking back at
~~~

what has happened, but I had never felt more alone. The room started closing in on me as tears ran down my red puffy face. With my face buried in my knees, I gave up feeling the pain and whimpered like I didn't every night for ten years. I did not know what to do at this point. But just then I heard a noise...

I took my face out of my knees and looked up. The noise chimed again and I looked over at the open window. Over by the window a small white bird chirping a little tune had perched itself on the window sill.. It stared at me with wonder. I could not help but smile at it. I got up and approached the window and the small winged creature just looked at me with those tiny black eyes. My hand reached out and it moved its little legs onto my palm, tickling me slightly with its tiny talons.. I gazed at it and it opened its tiny beak, like it was smiling. It was the cutest thing I have seen in an awfully long time. I settled it down and it looked at me one last time before beating its wings and taking flight.

I watched it soar and whipped my face. Something came over me and I realised I had to march into that school and face the music no matter the outcome. There was something about that bird that told me to stop being afraid of the past and run into the future. It was still early in the day but I dived into my bed and slept for hours. As afraid as

I was, it felt good to finally rest, and if I woke up in the underworld. So be it...

I had set an alarm before I slept and that was what I woke up to. I rubbed the sleep from my eyes and sighed with relief when I realized I was safe in my own bed. That feeling of safety was the best feeling after days of no sleep. It was 7:30 and the school day started at 9:00. I had to get ready for what could be one of the most important days of my life.

I showered, brushed my teeth, brushed my hair, dressed myself in the best clothes I had and marched out the door with my head held high. The school was only down the road so it didn't take me long to get there. It was 8:55 and I stood at the school gates paralyzed. I was so scared of walking into that building and immediately making a fool of myself. Many other students were gathered round the yard in groups and it was slightly intimidating. I walked towards the double doors into the school but they were locked. Ms. Noble wanted to meet me before I started the day and get me familiar with how things worked at the school. She said she would meet with me at 9:00. But then I started to think of the bad things that could happen. If I said something wrong, she could kick me out instantly. Maybe this wasn't such a good idea after all. I turned to leave but suddenly a very loud sound filled the school yard. It was a loud bell and everyone reacted. The double doors swung open and the hallways flooded with students. I was pushed and bumped into but I found safety in a doorway. I kept to myself until the corridors were clear. I was told to meet the principal at reception, so I followed the signs down the hallways.

Now that the halls were clear of students, I could see properly what it was like in the school. There were notice boards filled with 'motivational' quotes and upcoming events. I stopped and read one of the fliers that said, 'Hampton High Midterm Dance'. It sounded like the Founding Day ball my parents threw at the palace every year. The entire kingdom would get together to celebrate the founding of Atlasdam. It really showed the community of the realm. I hoped I would have that connection with people at this school. I might even make some friends.

I made my way to reception and there I saw Principal Noble and two other students my age. She saw me walking down the corridor and fixed the collar of her suit. I quickly fixed my long messy hair discreetly as possible and whipped the sweat from my face.

"Raven I presume?" she said and I immediately recognized her very posh voice.

"Yes, Raven Griffin" I responded and put my hand out, she shook it firmly.

"Welcome to Hampton High, where we believe you will be very happy here." she said and then indicated to the two other students with her.

They were a boy and a girl. The girl had soft dirty blonde hair and a bright face with piercing blue eyes that shined like sapphires. The boy was tall, tanned and very built. He had short dark brown hair and matching brown chocolate eyes.

"This here is Layla and Jack, two of our best students" she introduced them and they gently waved.

"Now, Layla and Jack will show you around because I am very busy, but I will meet with you later for a chat." she said and shook my hand again. "It was lovely to meet you and I hope you enjoy your time here." She trotted down a corridor, her heels clicking all the way.

Layla, Jack, and I started roaming around the school. It was a lot bigger than I thought.

"And this is where we will have a homeroom with Mr. Green," said Layla, opening the classroom door.

"He can be really odd sometimes but you get used to it." said Jack and chuckled.

They were being truly kind to me and I was really taken back by it. I was expecting everyone to think

I was a freak but I guess they couldn't really tell I was from another world.

"I just want to say thank you for this" I said, "I never really get treated like this." I immediately regretted saying that because I realized it was a really awkward thing to bring into a casual conversation.

"Don't worry about it dude. High school sucks, everyone has stuff going on." said Jack and patted me on the back.

"Yeah, we lost our parents two years ago and we have had each other's backs ever since." Layla said and Jack put his arm over her.

I couldn't believe they just shared that with me. Two people I have never met before just told me something I could relate to on an unimaginable level. Something I have mourned over and suffered with for 10 years.

"My parents are dead too..." I said with my nose to the ground.

The two of them came over to me and wrapped their arms around me. Their embrace was warm and full of delight. A bead of liquid formed in my eye but I caught it with my finger before it ran down my face.

"I already know we are gonna' be great friends

bro." said Jack.

The three of us spent the entire day together and I was the happiest I have been in a long time. They were in all my classes and we sat down for lunch and got to know each other more.

"My mom and dad were on my dad's boat and they got caught in a bad storm at sea. Then the waves got the better of them. So now my butler looks after me in my big empty house. I didn't even get a chance to say goodbye." Layla said and forced a smile across her face. I held out my hand and she held it tightly.

"Well, my dad went out with his friends one night and he never came home, and I never knew my mother. My uncle became my legal guardian but he's an alcoholic so I'm always at Layla's" he said and he didn't bat an eye. He didn't want to seem weak in front of the new kid but I didn't say anything. "What about you Ray'?"

My mind paused; slightly taken aback by the nickname they had just given me. What was I supposed to say to these guys? 'Oh yeah, I was forced to kill my evil mother corrupted by a strange snake's venom and my father probably died of a broken heart.' I needed a good substitute but my mouth came out with all kinds of stuff.

"Well...my mother was...murdered by this

psychopath in the street...and my father didn't last long after her death." I struggled to say.

They were both speechless, wide eyed and jaws dropped. I guess that kind of thing isn't very common here. I lowered my head but Jack patted my back again. Layla smiled and her white teeth sparkled. They hugged me again and this time I didn't fight the tears. For the first time in 10 years, I wasn't alone....

7

THE A.S DESTINY

~~~

I was beyond grateful to be blessed with two friends after all that has happened. A month has come and gone since I started school and I was doing well. Surprisingly, I was doing well at my classes and I have gotten closer to Layla and Jack. We have been spending time together every day after school and I treasured every moment of it. We would occasionally go to the coffee place...where Charissa's library was. At first, I wasn't okay with it, but gradually I began to get used to it. We got kicked out one time because we stayed after closing and laughed for ages about it. There were things I still didn't understand in this world, but the more time I spent with Layla and Jack, the more I understood. Without knowing it, they have shown me amazing things, things that I wouldn't never have thought of and things that made me realize that the whole universe isn't held together by magic. As much as I wanted to see my family again, as much as I desired to feel my mother and fathers embrace again, I was grateful for the place I was in.
~~~

The current school day was coming to an end and it was Friday, the weekend was nearly here. We had chemistry with Mr. Weldon and this was the first time I thought I saw actual magic in this world. Mr. Weldon poured water onto a shiny piece of metal in a glass, and suddenly the metal caught fire.

"That was so cool" I mouthed to Jack who was sitting beside me.

"You should have seen what he did last year. His entire fire face was covered in black powder." he told me and we both giggled.

The bell rang and everyone got to their feet and dashed out the door. The halls flooded with students, eager to get home and spend two days without school. I quite enjoyed school actually. It took my mind off everything and gave my brain a chance to expand. Layla and Jack, not so much. Just like everyone else, they were always excited when they heard the last ding at the end of the day. We had half days on Wednesdays so we would always go down to the coffee place and I would always try to forget what that place used to be...

We were all hungry so we made the unsaid decision to get food at a 'pizza place.' I had no idea what pizza was but it sounded unique. It was only a few blocks away from the coffee shop so it didn't take us long. Unfortunately, everyone else had the same idea and the cue was out the door. We waited patiently in line and luckily it was getting shorter by the minute. After what seemed like hours, we eventually made it to the front desk.

“Hi, what can I get you?” asked the lady enthusiastically.

Layla stepped up first and ordered her food. She said she wanted ‘pepperoni’ and ‘olives.’ I had no idea what that was but she seemed excited to get it. Jack was next and he ordered a plain ‘margarita.’ I had no idea what these words meant but I liked the sound of ‘margarita.’ I was next and I had no idea what to say to this woman.

She stood there smiling at me and stood there smiling back without saying a word. I didn’t know what pizza was let alone what kind to get. I eventually just said to her- “I’ll have what he’s having” and indicated to Jack.

“Ok, your total will be 8,95 please.” she said while tapping on a screen in front of her. I handed her the money and stood with Jack and Layla. The lady asked for my name, I told her and she said it will be ready in a few minutes.

While we waited for our pizza I offered to go back to my place and eat our food. The two of them were alright with that since it looked as though it was about to rain. After a few minutes, the lady called my name and for a split second I wondered how she knew my name but instantly copped onto myself. Our food came in these flat square boxes and it smelled divine. I couldn't wait to taste it but first we had to get back before we got soaked. So, we strolled in the bitter cold with the hot pizza warming our hands.

We got back just in time because when we got inside it started raining really bad outside. We sat down at the table and I grabbed some napkins and plates – which I had bought with my duplicated money, amongst other things. I opened my box and the aroma of the warm treat filled my nose. A delicious looking circle of yellow and red sat in the box and was divided evenly into eight pieces. I looked at Layla and Jack and they started pulling theirs apart and eating it with their hands. I did the same and dug in, and my tastebuds exploded. I have never tasted anything like this before and I adored it. The combination of cheese and tomato was exquisite. I devoured the entire thing and I enjoyed every bite. After a delicious few minutes, I leaned back in my chair and embraced the aftermath of the best meal I have had in over ten years.

"You certainly enjoyed that didn't you?" said Layla laughing, picking up the three boxes and disposing of them.

"Yeah, it was the best." I said and burped. "Excuse me." We all laughed but our heads turned to the window when we heard thunder outside. The rain was coming down even heavier now and the wind was strong enough to set an airship completely of course.

"Looks pretty bad out there," said Jack, slightly worried. "I don't think we should go walking home out in that."

"Well let's wait it out a bit longer and then we can decide what to do." said Layla coming from the kitchen. "Let me just call Chives." She started tapping on her phone then held it to her ear. There was a pause and then she grunted. "There's no signal...must be the storm."

We all sat down in the living room and waited out the storm. It was 11 o' clock and the storm was still shaking the trees and knocking over trash cans. We all knew that this was going to go on all night. I would have felt terrible if Jack and Layla walked home in that dangerous weather.

"Hey why don't you guys stay here tonight?" I asked.

"You sure Ray? I mean we could always call an uber." said Jack but I could tell he still didn't want to go out there.

"Yeah, sure it's no problem. But one of you will have to sleep on the floor."

Layla and Jack did something called 'rock, paper, scissors while I went down the hall to get some blankets and pillows. I opened a cupboard and heard Layla cheer so she must have won the couch. I found some blankets and pillows in the cupboard but they were covered in dirt and dust. I couldn't give them to my friends in that state. Then I had an idea. I waved my hand and recited a spell. My magic surrounded the bedclothes and suddenly they were clean. Whenever I had spare time, which I had a lot of, I would go and read some of the spell books in the basement. That spell was in a book called 'Simple spells Vol.1'. I kicked the cupboard closed and walked back down the hall.

"Hey heads up." I said and tossed a pillow at Jack. His reflexes were quite good and he caught it. "Layla, catch!" I tossed another pillow at her but it ended up hitting her on the head. "Sorry" I said and we both laughed.

"Jack's mad cus' he has to sleep on the floor." She whispered to me and we both giggled.

"You guys do know I can hear you right?" he said angrily

"Come on, it's only for one night," I said. "Then you can be at home in your own bed"

"Remember the school lock in and it was freezing!" she said to Jack. "Me and you huddled up in a corner to stay warm." said Layla trying to hold in a giggle.

"You were the one that forced me into that. Why in hell would I give up my Saturday to spend the night on the gym floor?" he complained

"Just get on the floor ya' big baby" she said and threw the blanket over him.

Jack grabbed the couch cushions and made himself and bed on the floor. Layla and I were about to move the couch to make room but just then it all went dark. The power had gone out. Jack grabbed his phone and turned on his flashlight.

"The storm" he groaned and shoved his face into his pillow.

I was fed up with this storm and just wanted to sleep through it. The heating had stopped working so I got more blankets for Layla and Jack because they were going to be freezing.

"You're gonna' need them" I said and walked down the hall to my room. "Night guys."

"Night!" They responded and I shut my door.

It was late and I was still awake. The storm was still restless outside and it kept me awake. My foot was out of the safety of my bed and I could feel a frigid air on my toes. I got up and could feel a cold breeze coming from inside the house. There must have been a draft. Wrapped in my duvet, I wandered the house looking for the source of the draft. Somehow Layla and Jack were able to sleep through the madness outside. After I checked all the windows and saw they were all closed, I had no idea how the cold was getting in. I stood in the living room trying to think but I felt the cold on my feet again. I got on my knees and felt around. The cold was coming from underneath the secret bookcase. My head glanced to see if Layla and Jack were actually asleep and they were out cold. I conjured my ball of light and opened the bookcase. I immediately felt the same cold on my face and it filled the room. This was where the cold was coming from.

I went down to the library to put a stop to this cold so I could go back to sleep in peace. My hand scanned the room with my light but I couldn't find the source of this wretched draft. I sat down in annoyance and rested my head on the bookcase. The lack of rest was getting to me and I just wanted to sleep but suddenly I felt the cold again on the back of my neck. It sent chills down my spine and I turned around to investigate. There was a crack in the back of the bookshelf and that's where the cold was coming from. I grabbed a book from a higher shelf to block it but the entire thing started to shake. Just like the bookcase in the living room, it started moving and revealed yet another secret room. Who built this place and what was their obsession with secret bookcases?

I walked into the room and the cold surrounded me. It was extremely dusty and I sneezed. The sneeze echoed in the dark room so it must have been big. I wandered the room and in the corner of my eye I saw a light. I walked towards it and as I got closer, I realized it was my own light reflecting off something metallic. It was a metal plate attached to a wall. It was dusty so I whipped it and engraved into it said 'A.S Destiny.' I had no idea what that was supposed to mean so I kept looking. I wandered a bit more and eventually reached the bookcase again. But when I walked out, I didn't realize the big switch on the wall. I pulled it down and one by one, lights illuminated the room, and what I saw next, nearly made me faint.

I couldn't believe what I was seeing. I smacked myself a few times to make sure I wasn't dreaming but this was reality. An Atlian airship stood right in front of me. The very thing that me and my friends would spend hours counting and watch as they flew by. I cried at the sight of it. This was my way home. This was here all this time and I never knew it. The ship was in a rough state but all I had to do was repair it and I would be able to fly home and reunite with my father. There was a book on dimensional travel in the library so I would be able to do my research. But then it hit me just like it did when I found the first secret room. Why was all of this here?! This world has no magic and no one needs to travel across the realms so why in the name of Zeus was there an entire Airship beneath the earth of the house that Charissa...

Charissa... She must have known about this somehow. And now she is gone. There was no way to ask her and make any sense of this. My mind was spinning and I had completely forgotten about finding the draft and going back to sleep. The pull of finding out the meaning of this was too much. There was a ladder nearby so I used it to climb up to the deck of the ship. When I got onto the ship, my foot went through the floor, just like when I first walked into the house. If I ever find the person that owns this house, I'm giving them a lesson on how to look after a house. This hunk of junk was going to need a lot of work if it was going to get in the air. There was a door to what must have been to the captain's quarters. I pushed the door open and it came off the hinges. The room was dark so I conjured my light once again. There was a desk in the middle of the room and behind it was an official looking, ripped up chair. On the desk was a manuscript. It was a journal, and in gold foil had two letters, T.S. I blew the dust off it and opened the journal.

"Day 1" it said. "We started our search in far corners of the realm to make sure they weren't still in Atlasdam."

So, this person was in Atlasdam and they were looking for someone. I continued to read.

“The king had chosen me himself to search for the young prince while he and his most trusted knights did their own search. When I left the city, I knew right then and there I wouldn’t not stop until he was found or until my king ordered me otherwise.”

My heart flooded with tears. I felt a spark of hope in my heart. My own father was searching every corner of the universe for me. But why didn’t he find me? I decided to flick to the very last entry of the journal to find out what happened.

“Day 2920” I quickly calculated in my head and realized this T.S person had searched for 8 years. The lump in my throat got larger as I continued to think about it. For eight years my father and his forces searched for me, but never did.

“I received a message from His majesty today. He wanted me to return to Atlasdam and stop my search. I am truly devastated that we never found young Raven, but I'm sure he’s not so young anymore, if he is even alive. The Destiny had taken too much damage so someone was coming to bring me back in a ship of their own. I have to leave all my books and belongings in this world but it will stay hidden in the secret room I built along with what is left of the Destiny.”

My heart dropped. They gave up...My father had called off the search and declared me dead. I couldn't believe what I was reading. For a moment I thought my father still cared. No, I thought. He does still care. All I had to do was fix this ship and show him that my blood still pumps. It might take a lot of work but I wouldn't give up until it was flight worthy. I climbed down off the ship and took one last look at it. The fire of hope relit in my heart and I was determined to show my father and everyone else that I was alive. I would have quite the story to tell.

"Raven?" said a voice

I jumped in fear and turned around.

It was Layla and Jack...

8

PREPARATIONS

~~~

"So let me get this straight. You're from another world another world, 'Atlydam'-

"Atlasdam." I corrected Layla.

"Yeah, so you're from another world. Your Mom turned evil and brought you to the underworld and was trapped there for ten years. You escaped in another one of these 'ships' and you were stuck here up until now, and this thing is gonna' get you back. Have I got that right?" she finished with her arms crossed and eyebrows raised.

"Yep, that sums it up pretty nicely." I said but the looks on their faces told me they weren't buying it.

"I'm not buying it." Jack exclaimed. "Where's the cameras cus' I know where on some episode of 'Gotcha.'

I had just finished telling them everything they didn't already know. About the gods, the other realms, and the traumatic things I experienced in
~~~

the last years.

I knew I had to show them who I really was. I held my hands out and conjured a glowing ball of red light. It appeared levitating in my hands as it shone all over the room and into Layla and Jack's eyes. They were dazzled and their mouths were open in amazement. They couldn't believe what they were seeing. I reached my hand again and pointed it at a table of tools in the corner of the room. I closed my eyes and channeled my power. The tools shone red and rose from the table. My hand moved and the tools moved with it. Wrenches and hammers danced above our heads at my command and the two were lost for words. I finished my little light show and looked at them for an answer.

"I think I believe you now...." Layla said breathlessly.

"Yeah, I don't see how you can do that with special effects." Jack said, still astonished.

The three of us headed back upstairs to sit down because they both looked like they were going to faint. I poured glasses of water for them and they finally looked like they were relaxed. I too would be shocked if everything I believed in was a lie. Discovering that your world is just one of many can be a bit overwhelming. But I had to make sure that Layla and Jack kept this all a secret. I sat down with them and begged them to not tell anyone about this. Not only would it probably get me hunted down by Area 51, but it would also make Layla and Jack look like they were on drugs.

"I mean if I told Tony that my friend is from another world and can make stuff fly round the room, he'd think I'm crazier than my uncle." said Jack laughing into his water.

"Thank you, guys, and thank you for being there for me when I had no clue what this world had in store."

They both laughed and smiled at me.

"Don't worry about it Ray. It's not like we did it on purpose." said Layla and we laughed again.

They had quite a few questions about the other worlds and the gods. I mean that's understandable but I seemed like I was there for hours answering their constant queries. We were there for so long that the sun rose and light shone into the room.

"So, if you fix up that piece of junk in the basement, you'll be able to sail home?" Jack asked.

I chuckled. "No, it's not going to sail, it's going to fly..."

Their eyes grew and their mouths dropped. "That things gonna fly?!" They both asked loudly.

"Yes, but not in the state that it's in. It's going to

need a lot of work."

"Well, what are we sitting around for?" Jack said and shot to his feet. "We need to get you home! You're lucky I got an A in wood-shop."

I smiled and a bead of liquid rolled down my face but I caught it before either of them noticed. "Thank you" I said and sniffed.

"Obviously, I'm in to." Layla exclaimed. "But can we sleep first and then get to work?"

We all agreed that was the best thing to do. I didn't get any sleep at all and we were going to need all the strength we had if we were going to get that ship flight worthy.

We slept for about 12 hours and they were 12 hours of pure joy, believe me. We woke up and headed down to see what the damage was on the ship. Well, the sail for starters was ripped to shreds, the rudder was nowhere to be seen and the mast was on the verge of collapse. Not to mention all the damaged wood and boards. Luckily, T.S was kind enough to leave some materials to work with, wood and nails and some other stuff.

"Are you sure we can get this thing working?" Layla asked without any enthusiasm.

"Not with that attitude we won't." I snapped "If we put in the effort and time then eventually it will fly." But suddenly there was a loud snap followed by a crash. The mast had collapsed. They both looked at me with an unhopeful look.

"I think we need more than time and effort. We need a miracle." Jack scoffed.

I didn't want to admit it to them but I wasn't very hopeful either, but I had to try. This was the one and only way I was going to get home. Either this or I live out my days without a family. I looked at it one more time before I said anything else. It was in really rough shape, but it was all I had.

"We can do this, and if we can't then that's it. There's nothing else we can do."

They both shared a look and sighed. They knew I was counting on them.

"Ok let's do it." Layla said and grabbed mine and Jack's hands.

"Thank you. You have no idea how much this means to me."

We began work with our heads held high and our sleeves rolled up. Over the next few weeks, we would come home from school and work on getting this hunk of junk in the air. Layla volunteered to sew up the sail while me and Jack started on the mast. It was really heavy but I used my magic to hold it in place while Jack nailed supports into it. Next, we had to fix all the floorboards. We took them out and replaced them one by one. A few splinters later we had the floor repaired. Jack put his knowledge of wood-shop to good use to make a new rudder since the previous one was nowhere to be found. After a few days we had a *like* new sail and rudder. After a long build session one night, we sat down and discussed some things over pizza.

"So, when we finally finish this thing, how exactly are you gonna' get home?" Jack asked, his mouth full of pizza

"Well, I thought about this while we were fixing the floor. In the library there's a book on dimensional travel. Before portal opening was discovered, people used the temples in every realm that houses the gateways to said realms. Zeus created these temples and connected all of them to allow passage between the known realms."

"So, anyone can just travel from world to world? Sounds a bit dangerous if you ask me." she said.

"No, the protector of the gateway is Hermes, the god of travel. He is the only one that can open the doors of the temples in every realm. But no one has heard from him in a long time since the gods can open portals whenever they want."

"So, is there one of these temples here on earth?"

"This T.S person left a bunch of maps on their ship. Luckily for me, they had one on earth, and on the map has the location of this world's gateway temple."

Layla and Jack stopped eating and looked at each other. Jack nodded indicating something but I had no idea what was going on.

"Raven, me and Jack have been talking, and we wanted to ask you something..."

I sat in confusion; my mouth was full of soda. "Okay?"

"Me and Layla wanted to know if..." They shared one last look. "If we could come with you...to Atlasdam."

I spat out my soda all over the table. I wiped my mouth and spoke.

"Are you guys serious?"

They nodded and waited for a serious response.

"You guys want to leave this world behind, where you understand everything and want to enter a completely new one where you won't know anything."

They nodded again.

"Jack, what about your uncle?"

"What about him? He doesn't even care about me! All he cares about is the bottle. The only class I'm passing is wood-shop and I don't have any parents. So yeah, I would drop everything to go off to an unknown world."

"And I get bullied for being the rich girl with no parents. My butler expects me to be this posh lady and eat all these really disgusting foods. Raven, it's pretty obvious neither of us are happy in this world so of course, we would run away from it all to a brand-new world where we can see new things and start fresh."

I never thought someone would want to run away from the very place they grew up in. All this time I wanted to get home and I guess I never thought someone could be unhappy in their homes. In fairness, I did grow up underground, isolated from society. But I was glad that they had told me, otherwise I would have flown off and abandoned them. I knew what I had to do.

"Of course, you can come with me. We started this as a team, and we will end this as a team. Let's finish this and go home."

"Thanks man. You are giving us the chance no one else could." Jack bawled.

"We are with you to the very end Raven." Layla sobbed.

We finished everything that needed to be done and everything was ship shape. But there was one final task. The most important thing needed to be added to accomplish our mission. Remember how I said that Airships run off magic? Well, the engine literally runs on magic. The engine room powered the whole ship. And that needed to be powered with every ounce of strength I had if it was going to fly us to Atlasdam. This was going to drain me big time. I held my hands out and channeled my power harder than I ever had before. I fueled the ship with the magic from my blood and felt my own life force pump through the ship. The very essence of my vigor escaped my body and entered the veins of the aircraft. After I felt it was powered enough, and I couldn't supply anymore, I cut all power and I fell to the floor. I felt lifeless and didn't even have the strength to stand. Jack and Layla put my arms around their shoulders so I could get to my feet. Now was the moment of truth.

We headed up to the helm of the ship and Jack pulled the long lever. The ship woke up from its long slumber and sparked to life. It rose from the ground and Jack shut it off before it went through the roof. I screamed in pure happiness because I knew I was finally going home. Layla jumped on me and squeezed the life out of me. We were so proud of what we had accomplished.

We packed up our things onto the ship and

prepared to take flight. We sat outside my house one last time and took in the surroundings we knew we wouldn't see again. We knew this would be the last time we would see this town and this entire world. I took one last deep breath through the nose and I heard a small noise. I looked around and I heard it again. I felt a poking at my leg and I looked down to see something familiar. It was my little bird friend from the window in all its white feathered glory. It chirped its little tune and it was like it knew what was about to happen. I decided to name him. He was quite a chirpy little thing and that's when I came up with the idea to call him Chip. He was very attached to me because he flew onto my shoulder and refused leave. Layla thought maybe we should take him with us and I didn't see any problem with that. It's always nice to have an animal companion.

We were all set to leave, and I couldn't have been happier. Jack and Layla were taking it pretty hard and I comforted them while they made this hard decision.

"Are you guys sure you still want to go?"

They both hesitated to speak but eventually they both nodded and didn't look back. We waited until nightfall so no one would see a giant flying ship. We all boarded the now repaired airship. I pulled down the lever to open the hangar doors above us and the ship rose out from the underground.

Whoever built this place really thought of everything. We flew higher and higher until I knew the moment was right.

"You guys ready for this?" I asked excitedly.

"Wait!" Layla called out. "I think we should do something first!" She pulled her phone from her pocket and looked at me and Jack.

We both then knew what had to be done. We pulled out our own phones and looked at each other.

"Ok," Layla breathed. "Three, two, ONE!" she shouted and all three of us threw our phones as far as we could into the ocean and watched as they plopped into the water and sank. It may have not been very good for the environment, but that feeling of not having to worry about having a phone constantly was sort of reliving. They weren't going to work once we entered the temple so what else were we going to do with them.

"Are we ready now?!" I called out again

"YEAH!" They both cheered

"Better hold onto something" I said with a grin.

We all braced ourselves and then I grabbed the accelerator, lunging it towards me. The ship took off at great speed across the ocean. We were off.

Into the great beyond...

9

THE GREAT BEYOND

~~~

The feeling was surreal. The wind in my hair and to smell the fresh sea air of freedom. For the first time in years, I was truly free. To feel that I was finally going home and I had new friends to experience it with, was surreal to say the least. Layla and Jack were still blown away by the fact the ship could fly. Even my new companion Chip was excited. He loved to sit on my shoulder or relax in the pocket of my hoodie. It was nice having him around. We glided across the seas and made our journey to the gateway temple. I wasn't an expert cartographer but I think I was reading the map correctly. According to T. S's map, the temple was smack in the center of the Atlantic Ocean. I just hoped that Hermes was still there and would be able to help us. We come all this way and he is not there? Who knows what I will do?

Two days into our voyage and we were only halfway there according to the map. But we didn't care, we were having the time of our lives. We all
~~~

imagined what it would be like when we inevitably returned to Atlasdam. I told them all about it and they were giddy with excitement. They adored hearing about the other worlds and all the wonders that lived within them. I told them about the people, the animals, the nature...and that it was all real. That they too would be able to witness it all for the first time, just like I did.

"Are we nearly there yet?" they asked me constantly.

After a while I was able to say "Yes, almost there."

"What are we going to do if it's not there?" Jack asked.

"We will cross that bridge when we come to it..." We hated thinking about the fact that we would get there and there might be nothing. But I had hope, and right now, that was all I needed.

We were nearly there and I was about to pass out with the tension. I pushed the lever and the ship came to a stop. Layla and Jack looked out onto the empty waters in confusion.

"So where is it?"

"Hermes had a protection spell put in place so human voyagers wouldn't stumble upon the temple by accident. There's a counter spell I have to recite."

In the book of dimensional travel there was a spell. I opened it up and recited the words. As every letter escaped my lips, I felt the atmosphere around me change. I looked down at the water and the very sea started to erupt. Waves crashed against each other and something started to rise from beneath the ocean.

“It's working!” Layla cheered.

I continued to gaze at the water as the temple rose but suddenly, I realized a horrible truth. In the book it mentioned a guardian, a beast of immense power that was said to guard the temple.

“Raven, I'm no expert on temples, but I don’t think that’s it....”

Layla was all to right. A giant tentacle rose from the water and another one followed it. One by one, tentacles surrounded us and then rose the beast itself. The Leviathan...protector of earth's gateway...

Its size was bigger than a building. Its eyes were like two boulders. And its teeth were like stalagmites. The three of us were frozen with fear as we stood motionless in the presence of the titan. I bucked up the courage to move and yanked the ship's accelerator and it jolted into action. The Leviathan reacted and swung its colossal tentacle at the aircraft but I spun the wheel and just dodged it.

“Raven don’t you think you could have told us

about the giant octopus before we agreed to come on a life-or-death journey?!" Layla screamed, holding onto dear life.

"I'm sorry, I didn't think it would still be alive after all these years! I thought someone would have killed it by now!"

"Who the hell could have killed that thing let alone get past it!"

I panicked immensely and I suddenly started getting flashbacks. I began seeing Medusa instead of the Leviathan. I found myself back in the underworld flying a ship for my life, running from a titan. My sight was dizzy, zoning in and out, the ear-piercing screams of Medusa wouldn't stop in my mind. I couldn't get trapped again, I wouldn't. The fear was dragging me down and I collapsed to my knees, losing control of the ship. I felt Chip restless in the pocket of my hoodie and held onto him as I tried to steer us away from the danger. The beast swung its tentacle again and knocked me right off the deck of the ship, Jack and Layla screaming my name. I held onto chip as I fell through the air, my trauma flashing before me, tears waving down my face. Some may say that the water would save you, but when you fall from that height, it's basically solid concrete. This was it.

"I'm sorry father. I failed you."

The ocean was getting closer and I prepared for my passing, but then Chip started pecking at me. I pulled him out and he looked at me with his little eyes. I closed my eyes and accepted my fate. I was about to plummet to my death in the smothering intensity that was the ocean. But nothing happened, I was alive.

I opened my eyes and I was above the water, floating. I could fly! I looked at Chip and he was alright. I settled him back in my pocket and tried to get my balance. I stumbled a few times but I got the hang of it. The beast was still after my friends, so I flew up to help him. Jack took control of the ship and I tried to steer it away from the Leviathan. The beast swung its giant tentacle at the ship, about to crush it, but I swooped in and casted a shield to protect my friends. They were both in shock to see me still alive. I looked at them with a look of assurance and they sprang into action. Layla fastened the sails and Jack held the helm with all his strength.

“I have an idea,” I said as I flew beside the ship.

“Let's hear it because any idea is good one right now.” said Layla still panicking

“I say we use its size against it.” I explained. “Just stay on your toes and follow me.”

“Roger that captain.” Jack said and saluted me.

I dove under the beast's arched tentacle with the Destiny right behind me. I felt more alive than ever, like we could actually do this. We flew over and under this obstacle and rose face to face with it as it stared at me with deadly intentions. It swung its tentacle from behind us once again and we dodged it, causing it to collide with the titan, knocking itself out completely. It froze for a second and then fell back into the sea.

I floated down to the Destiny and we all sat still trying to catch our breath after facing that ordeal.

"Is everyone okay?" I said and leaned back onto the helm.

Jack gave me a thumbs up and Layla called out as she leaned over the side, throwing her guts up.

"So, you can fly now huh?" Jack forced a laugh through his heavy panting.

"Add that to the list of things I didn't know I could do."

"What do we do now?" Layla asked green as grass.

She had a point. I thought if we defeated the Leviathan the temple would show itself. Layla suggested that I say the spell again. I took the book out and recited the spell once again. I looked down at the water and it started to churn. I prayed to Zeus that the terrible thing wouldn't wake up, but I caught a glimpse of a building beneath the surface of the water rise. I was sweating with the tension as the waves fought one another. The structure continued to rise; my wish came true...

"Ladies and gentlemen, we have reached our destination. Welcome to the Gateway Temple my friends." I said as it rose behind me.

The temple was bigger than I had ever imagined. The area it covered was about the size of a small housing estate and it was taller than the empire state building. It was built out from other worldly turquoise brick and was surrounded by giant arches, almost resembling the tentacles of the Leviathan. The entrance of the temple was big enough for the Destiny to fly through. We proceeded with caution because who knows what could jump out at us.

We flew down the titanic hallways of the temples and we all felt like ants in a big house. It was dimly lit by blue lamps that floated around like fireflies in the night. There were Illustrations of the gods and magical animals decorated the walls of the interior of the temple. It was telling a story of some sort. There was a drawing of a bearded man next to an explosion. So that must have been Zeus and the big bang. Next there was the same big bang surrounded by worlds. So that must have been him creating the realms. We slowly cruised through the temple but made sure to keep up with the depictions. The last one we saw of the bearded man- Zeus- was him laying down in a tomb of some sort in a realm I wasn't familiar with.

My father told me that no one knows where Zeus's final resting place is and that most people silently agreed that it should remain a secret. Although there are people that search for it to claim the rumored 'treasure' that he left, but no one has been successful. Layla and Jack's eyes were glued to the walls; they were so fascinated by the history of the realms. I told them everything I could as we looked at the drawings and they listened to every word of it.

We continued to fly through but I noticed something interesting. There was a depiction of a war between two realms, one good, one evil. The evil one had large wings and long horns that perched from two sides of his forehead. I soon realized that was none other than my own father, Triton. This was the war between my mother and father. I continued along the wall and the next portrayal was Atlasdam. My home.

"That's Atlasdam." I pointed out.

"That's where we're going?" they asked

"It sure is," I said, still looking at it.

But that wasn't it, it kept on going. There was my birth celebration, me growing up, and then my heart stopped. A portrait of me in Medusa's clutches in the underworld. The fear in my eyes and evil in hers was horrifyingly accurate. Jack and Layla repeatedly asked me what was wrong but my blood was boiling. My hands were on fire and my magic was reacting to my rage. I felt power run through me as the rage took hold. I blasted my power at the portrait and it was destroyed. A gaping hole was left where the portrait was, blacked a charred. Layla and Jack looked at me quite startled.

"What the hell did you do that for?!" Jack shouted at me.

"No, the better question is who the hell thought it would be a good idea to represent my biggest nightmare in one of universe's most sacred places!" I shouted furiously

"You need to control your anger; you never know when you could blast one of our heads off! "Layla exclaimed

"Look I'm sorry it's just something I'll never get over. I was getting flashbacks when we're facing the Leviathan and the screams in my head just wouldn't stop...and..... I saw her again."

They both came over and hugged me. "You know you can talk to us about anything, even though we don't understand everything. It's good to let it all out sometimes." Layla explained. "We may not be blood, but right now we are all family."

I hugged for a bit more then continued down the temple. After a few minutes we reached a giant room that I recognized as the gateway room itself. We finally made it. The room was shaped like a big octagon, and in every wall was a large door to a different world. In the middle of the room was a large flat wheel, this must be how Hermes opens every realm. The book said that every time a new realm is discovered, Hermes would add a new gateway into the room so others could access that realm. But there was one thing missing from it all, Hermes himself. He was nowhere to be found. We all called out his name and it echoed through the lifeless temple. We tried turning the wheel but it wouldn't budge. I started panicking again and frantically paced round the room trying to think of an alternative.

"What are we going to do? What are we going to do?"

"Hey that big door over there is open" Jack called out.

Layla and I darted over to where Jack was and he was right. All the other doors were closed while this one remained open. We couldn't see beyond the light that shone from the gateway so we had no idea where it led it to. Along the path up to the open door was this a big symbol on the ground. It was a magical looking leaf with vines intertwined with it, like a crest of some sort. There was only one thing we could do. Behind this door was a realm. So, there must be a god that ruled this realm that could help us.

"Into the great Beyond?"

10

THE REALM OF NATURE

~~~

Trees. Miles and Miles of trees and greenery. We had just gone through the gateway into this unknown realm and were welcomed by a warm atmosphere. The Ecosystem was nothing like I had ever seen. The nature was unparalleled to any other realm, it was beautiful. It was like an expanded version of the gardens in Atlasdam. This is where all the plants from the gardens must have come from. The grass was soft beneath our feet and whistled when the gentle breeze blew through it. The light shone through the tall pink leafed trees, creating spotlights all over. And the flowers had more variety than coffee on earth, and that's saying something. There were tall flowers, small flowers, magical flowers and much more.

We left the A.S Destiny at the temple and continued on foot. We wandered through the woods and the further we got the more we saw. But we didn't just see plants and flowers, we also encountered an animal. In a big patch of grass, we saw a deer frolicking, but it wasn't like any normal
~~~

deer. Its antlers where tall and blues rose sprouted from them, long reeds of grass dangling from them. His back legs were like thin tree trunks and he had a pair of wings, long majestic wings and seemed to resemble moss. The three of us hid in a bush and watched it quietly. Layla tried to get up and get closer but Jack held her down, he didn't want her to scare it. After a bit of struggle, she broke free of his grasp and slowly approached the winged creature. Chip tried to escape my pocket but I held him tightly and watched Layla. The deer noticed her and stood still, its eyes watching her every move. She was like a predator about to pounce, but scaring it was the last thing she wanted to do. Watching her footing, she walked as carefully as possible and put her hand out. The deer noticed her, got skittish, opened its long wings, and took off to the skies. Layla, disappointed, crossed her arms and sulked for the rest of the journey. Me and Jack watched the beautiful creature flap its majestic wings and dance through the air. Yet another feature of this realm. After a while we considered turning back and flying over the forest on the ship. We all agreed that was best and headed back.

A little while later we could see the temple past the trees but we stopped when we started hearing voices coming from the temple. The closer we got the clearer the voices became. We saw a group of people gathered next to the Destiny and we hid behind the trees. We peaked our heads around the trunks and realized we had a big problem. They were soldiers, all mounted on antlered horses. They were all dressed in suits of armor made of a strange green metal and a hard looking wood. There were about fifteen of them so we couldn't just charge at them. There was one soldier I had my eye on. He was tall and built, with a bald head and green face tattoos. He loomed over everyone on his massive antlered horse, which was armored itself. He must have been the one in charge. He was very menacing looking and the other men took his orders swiftly.

"There's no one on board captain." One of them reported from the ship.

"They must be around somewhere. Mistress Serenity sensed three life forms come through the gateway. They can't have gone far, but for now we take this ship back to the castle." Ordered the captain.

The captain led them away from the gateway and the knights in the ship flew above them.

"We have to follow them." I told Layla and Jack

They both looked at me as if I was crazy. "Raven I know we fought a giant octopus back there and all but if we get caught, we might get executed or something." Layla said genuinely concerned about my antics.

"This "Mistress Serenity" must be the god of this

realm. Maybe she might be able to get us home."

"Yeah, but what if she doesn't? What if we ask for help and she's insane?"

"Do you want to get Atlasdam or do you want to spend the rest of your days here in this forest?" I sarcastically asked and began following the soldiers while the other two hesitated, but eventually followed me.

We hid behind trees and in bushes as we followed the trotting antlered horses. The knights flying the Destiny followed from above, so we had to be careful they didn't see us either. A few minutes of ducking and peaking our heads, we made it to a road. The soldiers continued along this path which made it harder for us to hide. There were a few trees dotted on each side of the road but not as many. Since we were on the road, there were citizens on carts and horses. The people of this realm all had magical features about them that were similar to the realm they lived in. One person had green vines for hair, thorns for fingernails and bright pink skin, like a rose. Obviously, people from other realms look different but I have never seen people look quite like this.

We tried to think of our next move because the entrance to the city was getting closer. Jack noticed a cart being pulled by an antlered horse and Layla and I knew where he was going with this. He jumped up onto the cart and ducked down so the carter guiding the horse wouldn't notice him. Layla and I carefully followed him and stealthily jumped on the cart. There were some old rags covering barrels filled with fruit. We grabbed them and hid under them, trying to be as quiet as possible. I revealed my head from under the rag to see what was going on. I examined the gate for a way in incase this plan failed. There were two tall towers standing on either side of the large metal gate. They casted long shadows as they stood in front of the cool sun. Guard's stations themselves along the walkway between the two towers and on the ground as well. Connected to the towers stood a brick wall which seemed to go on for miles. It ran around the perimeter of the city, stopping unwanted guests I presumed.

The legion of soldiers ahead of us halted at the gates. The captain gave a signal to a guard at the gate and that guard yelled to another atop the tower. The gate lifted and the horses trotted into the city. The clip clop of the horses remained as the carter steered his own to the city entrance. The gatekeepers stopped the carter from going any further. I covered myself again and listened.

"What ya' got in that cart." The guard bellowed.

"Oh, just some fresh fruits I gathered from the south. It's all for the marketplace." The carter explained. He spoke softly and very relaxed, as if he knew for sure if was going to be granted entry.

“Going to have to search it.” The guard grunted.

The three of us held our breaths and prayed. If he finds us, it's game over. The tension grew inside us as the guard approached the cart.

“Let the guy pass, I have seen him before.” Another guard called out from above.

“Thank you very much my friend!” The carter called back. He whipped the reins on his antlered horse and it trotted through the gate into the city.

We all poked our heads up from under the rag to take a look at the new civilization we now found ourselves in. The carter rode down a narrow street with houses on either side of it. They were small and cozy looking, being made out of brick and wood, with thatched roofing. Everywhere you looked there was greenery. Flowers, ferns, rose bushes, if you name it, it was there. The carter brought his cart to a stop in an alleyway and started feeding his horse. Layla, Jack, and I jumped out and dashed behind a pile of bright blue radishes.

We sat down to catch our breath and to think of what to do next. There was one thing we had to take care of before we did anything. We needed to get a more casual attire so we wouldn’t attract any unwanted attention. Our earth jeans and hoodies weren't exactly normal for this world. We grabbed the rag from the cart and ripped it up enough to cover our earthly clothes. We looked just like any other common riff raff. We moved out onto the street and blended in.

The city was full of life and it had a welcoming atmosphere. There were no guards to intimidate the weak or prowl on the unfortunate. We came across the market place the carter was talking about. It was remarkably similar to one in Atlasdam. Everyone was friendly to one another and all was peaceful. It was like one big family. But I couldn't focus on that right now, I had to focus on getting back to my own family. From the street we could see the castle in all its glory. It stood atop a hill at the north side of the city. I saw the A.S Destiny fly towards it and land somewhere behind its walls.

"Those thieves better not damage my ship."

"Is that seriously the most concerning thing in your mind right now!?" Jack snapped. I was taken aback by this; I have never really seen him mad before.

"What's your problem?" I asked.

He ignored me and turned his head. Layla looked at me, confused as I was. We wandered the town for a bit more and we found ourselves in an exceedingly popular area. It was large and open, like the football pitch back at school, except there weren't stands or aggressive teenagers. It must have been the city square. There were trees dotted where people tended to sit under and relax, and hanging from those trees were bright yellow fruits. They were like apples but they were yellow and didn't look edible. They probably served as decoration. But in the middle of it all stood a monumental stone statue. It was of a beautiful woman dressed in a floral dress with magical flowers. She looked like a god. Many people gathered around her and prayed, throwing flower petals into the small moat that flowed around it.

"That must be her, Serenity, the god of this world."

"She's beautiful. I would be surprised if she wasn't considered a Goddess." Layla said gazing at the statue.

"'Fertility, our Goddess of Nature and Savior.'" Jack read aloud. "Says right here." He indicated some lettering in-grooved into the stone path. "Founded our glorious realm Leafstonia, 500,000 years after Zeus's passing. Fighting in the war alongside Rhea, the Goddess of love against the ruthless Triton, God of Revenge. After succeeding her mission to stop Triton, she returned and to this day, has never failed to protect our home from those who seek its destruction.'"

"So, Serenity isn't the god of this world?" Layla asked.

"Seems like it. The Goddess of Nature is Fertility, and she knew my mother so she might know me. But the one question remains, whose Serenity?" I wondered

"YOU THREE, HALT!" We looked behind us and about 10 guards charged in our direction.

"Are they coming after us?"

"Certainly, it looks like it! Let's get outta' here!"

We dashed across the square down into the streets again and the guards were hot on our trail. At least we knew that they were after us now. We darted into an alleyway and Jack kicked over a stack of barrels to slow down the guards. I levitated the other two over a wall and flew over myself. I continued running while looking behind me but fell to the floor after bumping into Jack.

"Why did you guys stop?" I looked up and they had both been stopped themselves. In front of them was the captain. Busted.

11

SERENITY

~~~

The guards had us cuffed and dragged us to the castle on foot. Everyone in town had their eyes on us. The guard took our rags so everyone could see our earthly clothes and see that we were not of this world. Layla and Jack kept looking at me as if I had an idea to get out of this mess. The sad truth was that I had no idea what to do. I tried to use my magic but it was like they had been zapped away.

"Don't bother trying to use your magic to fly out of here. Those cuffs are made of Magestone, cutting off all magic from the wearer, even gods." The captain explained. His voice was deep but he spoke softly. He was very intimidating as he walked, his long shadow casted onto us.

"Where are you taking us?" I demanded.

"The queen wants a word with you." he said with his back still turned to us. "After she sensed you come through the gateway and we found that piece of junk of yours, we knew you would go prowling
~~~

through the city like stray dogs."

"Hey buddy, we just crossed an entire ocean, defeated a giant octopus thing and made it to another world. So don't think we will hesitate to-" Layla elbowed Jack.

"Listen we don't want any trouble; we just came through the portal looking for help but then you took our ship!" She explained.

"Tell it to the Queen, she will want to hear all about your little adventure." He mocked.

It was getting dark as the day came to an end. The three of us hadn't slept in hours but we had to keep our eyes open for just a little longer. We were about to come face to face with a god and I wanted to make the best first impression. We stopped at a grand gate before the castle. There was another long, tall wall that wrapped around the perimeter of the castle but it looked even more secure than the one at the city entrance. The captain signaled to a guard on the gate and the whole thing opened. We all marched in as the gate closed behind us. If we thought the city was full of nature it was nothing compared to what grew in the castle gardens. There were astonishing looking trees that grew in ways I couldn't even think of. It spiraled like a fountain and now that it was dark, I could see the purpose of the yellow fruits. They shone bright in the night and it made the tree even more magical. As much as I wanted to sit and gaze at the wonders of the courtyard, the guards were shoving us along.

We entered the castle and it was truly nature incarnate. Vines swirled up the log pillars holding up the roof. More glowing fruit hanging from a chandelier made of twigs, and the amazing aroma of the flowers that grew in plant pots made from the stumps of trees. It was a long corridor of tension and suspense. We stood at a big pair of doors waiting for the moment we had been waiting for. Behind these doors was the person that could help us, or imprison us forever. The guards swung the doors open and we entered the throne room.

There wasn't a single soul in the room, apart from a small furry creature laying on the throne. The throne was made from a large tree, similar to the one outside. We approached the throne and the small creature looked up at me. It was a dog of some sort. It had fur like grass and its ears were simply two maple leaves. Chip flew out of my pocket and the creature started barking at him, and that's when someone walked into the room. It was a girl...A young girl.

The girl looked around my age. She walked in as if she owned the place. She wore a short gown made of red leaves. Her long blonde hair was tied up in vines and she wore a tiara made of intertwined twigs. Her bright green eyes and her skin was so clear as it reflected in the light of the glowing fruit.

"Leximus calm down." The girl said. She lifted the dog up and sat down on the throne with the dog on her lap. She slowly stroked it as she looked dead into my soul." So, these are realm hoppers I sensed. Is that right Darius?" She asked.

"Yes, my lady." the captain said bowed. So that was his name, Darius.

"You have some nerve entering a realm without clearance in these times. State your business now." she demanded.

Jack, Layla, and I looked at each other in confusion.

"When the Queen asks you a question, you answer it you filth!" Darius yelled.

"I'm sorry but you're the Queen?" I questioned. "It said outside by the statue that the Goddess of Nature, Fertility, is the Queen. "

The Girl smiled and chuckled. "You really have no idea, do you?" We all looked at her waiting for an answer. "I am Serenity, the daughter of Fertility."

"So where is Fertility?"

Serenity's face no longer shone. She looked almost sad at my question. "She can't be here right now." she said as she swallowed her pride. "While I watch over Leafstonia your fate is in my hands. So give me one good reason why I shouldn't have you locked up at this very moment."

"We're from earth and we're trying to get back to Atlasdam." I explained. "I'll save you the long boring story but we need to get there, it's the only thing I live for now..." I said and I lowered my head.

"Atlasdam you say? Explain yourself." Serenity demanded once again.

I told her my story. Why I ended up on earth in the first place, how I managed to get to the gateway and why we were doing all this. She was hooked on every word of it. But I was hooked onto what Serenity said previously.

'-in these times.' What did she mean by that?

"So, your father is Triton, former God of revenge, and your mother is Rhea, former Goddess of love, now dead, am I correct?"

I nodded. "I just want to get home. Can you please help us?" I begged. All my dignity had left my soul. All I have done, all the pain I have felt, the lives I lost, the monsters I've seen, I didn't care anymore.

She smiled and snapped her fingers. The cuffs binding our hands disintegrated and the magic flowed through me again.

"Walk with me"

The four of us strutted the halls of the castle and talked. I felt at ease with Serenity, but I also kept my guard up, she could pull anything at this time. But then again, if she really wanted to do anything to me, she would have left the handcuffs on. Chip sat on my shoulder while Serenity's Dog crawled behind us.

"It's a Leafstonian Vermillion, the last of its kind." she pointed as the pup licked my ankle. "She likes you."

"What did you mean by, In these times?" I asked.

Serenity took a big breath and leaned on a window sill. "My mother was taken. It happened two months ago. My mother heard some distressing news from another realm, but she refused to tell me what it was. She locked me in my room that night and she used her powers to protect me, but from what, I had no idea. Later that night I heard my mother scream from her room but I couldn't get out to see what was going on. But then the screaming stopped. My mother's magic on my room faded away and I could escape. I ran down the halls, her room empty; her window open and through it I could see a portal closing. We haven't heard from her since." Serenity sorrowed again but covered it up with a forced smile.

I put my hand on her shoulder and gave her a supporting smile. "When I landed on earth, I had no hope of seeing my father again. But when I found the A.S Destiny, that was the spark that lit the fire of hope again. What I'm saying is that you will see your mother again."

"I really wish I could help you Raven; I really do. Your mother and mine were very close. But without the Godly powers of my mother, we can't open a portal to leave the realm."

Layla and Jack looked at me in disbelief. "Is she serious?" Jack snapped. "Are we really stuck here?"

"What about the Gateway? Is there a way we can change what Gateway is opened?" I asked Serenity.

She pondered for a moment looking out the window. "Well, maybe If you and I combined our powers, we might be strong enough to turn the wheel and change the Gateway. But I'm not sure."

"Well, it's worth a try, isn't it?" Layla chimed in.

"I'll do it, for Layla and Jack." I said and turned to Serenity. "Are you in?"

She turned and gave us an eager look. "Alright, but if this goes south, don't blame me."

We had a plan. Serenity could control earth and the plant life around her. She would wrap vines around the Gateway Wheel while I used my magic to turn it also. It would take an awful lot of strength but it was a hard effort I was willing to make. If I can power a ship to travel over an entire ocean, then I'm sure I can turn a wheel. But I have only used my magic a few times so I had to train up. Every day I would go out and try to lift rocks off the ground as they gradually increased in size. Serenity would wrap vines around me and I would have to escape. She was always so pleased when I couldn't escape and she would have to let me go. Layla would always sit on the side and watch us train, but Jack would never show up for some reason.

I went to approach him about it one day but he was nowhere to be found. I asked one of the guards if they had seen him and he told me that every day he would disappear with Captain Darius. Then when I was going to get ready for training, I saw Jack and Darius in the courtyard. I flew over and hid behind the twisted tree to watch what was going on. They were fighting, with swords. Jack was actually able to hold his own against the big guy. After a strong strike from Darius, Jack was knocked to the floor. Darius held out his hand and pulled Jack up. I realized they weren't really fighting; it was civil between them.

After their session I approached Darius and he explained that Jack requested training of his own. He wanted to know how to handle himself against the average person from the other Realms. I mean I wasn't mad but I was just confused why he wouldn't tell us and why he kept it a secret. I decided to forget about it for the time being and focus on my training.

I felt like I was ready for the biggest rock after so much time and effort, and this rock was nearly as big as the twisted tree. I braced myself and held out my hands. With my mind open and thoughts clear, I imagined the rock coming off the ground. Determination strengthened me as I felt power flow through me. My red aura surrounded the rock and it began slowly rising. The density of the rock dragged me down but I was stronger than some rock. I yelled in frustration as the weight pulled at my might. There was no way I was going to let an overgrown pebble get the better of me. I used every drop of my magic stronger than I ever had before and cracks started to form within the stone. I could faintly hear Serenity screaming at me: stop! But rage clouded my judgement and ignored her cries. I used more and more of my power until more and more cracks formed and...I destroyed the rock...

Everything stopped. The pressure and the struggle snapped away. I fell to my knees and looked at the others. Their faces said it all. Layla dropped the book she was reading. Jack couldn't even form a word, and Serenity was struggling to close her mouth. Even Chip looked shocked as he sat on Leximus's head. Maybe I went a bit too far.

"Are you insane? Again?" Layla said, still shocked,

swiping the dust of her aggressively

“You mean to tell me he’s done this before?!” Serenity asked staggered.

“He blasted a mural of Medusa in the Gateway Hall. Left a giant hole in the wall.” Jack said and stormed off.

I attempted to get to my feet but the fatigue overcame and fell back to the ground. Layla and Serenity gathered round me to see if I was alright, but I fell out cold asleep. All my energy was zapped from me so all my body could do was fall into a deep slumber. They knew it would take a few days before my strength returned, so for now, they let me rest.

12

EMOTIONS

~~~

I slept for two days straight after the whole rock crushing incident. I hadn't felt that tired since I landed on earth and was awake for several hours. But I had to admit I wished I could have slept a little longer because the beds in the castle were astonishingly comfortable and cozy. The mattress was a smooth cotton that slid along your skin and the duvet was made of a soft moss that was never too cold or too warm. When Layla woke me up, I refused to leave that dream of a bed, but she ended up dragging me out herself. But as amazing the sleep had been, I had an odd dream. I wouldn't really call it a dream as I only heard voices and not images. It was a female voice speaking to me in a playful but direct manner. It told me "Find me Raven. Find me and we can do this together..." It almost sounded familiar to me but then again, I couldn't put my finger on who it could have been. I told the others about my dream and they told me that's all it was, a dream, and there was nothing I could do about it. But they told me what I could do was make final preparations before we set off.
~~~

That afternoon, I headed out to the courtyard to do some last-minute training but that's when I saw Jack. He was sparing Darius but this time he had really improved. Darius swung his blade at Jack but he swiftly leaned back to dodge it and tripped Darius with his leg. Jack held out his hand and pulled Darius to his feet and they shook hands.

"You're coming along great boy. You remind me of me when I was your age, beating everyone else and always coming out on top."

"I don't think I'll reach your level dude. But I enjoy this."

"Then why do you wish to keep this a secret? Why haven't you told your friends you have been training with me?"

Jack had a look of guilt on his face. He turned his back to Darius and sheathed his sword.

"You agreed that you would keep this between us. So, I don't see the big deal in telling them."

Darius put his hand on Jack's shoulder and turned him around. He looked into his eyes and I knew that he could see Jack's true intentions.

"My father once told me boy, "No man is weak, if he has friends to make him strong." Darius quoted.

Jack lowered his head and broke away from

Darius's gaze and walked away. Once Jack was nowhere to be seen, I approached Darius.

"What's going on with him?" I asked.

"My apologies but he asked me not to tell anyone."

"Did you offer to train him or did he ask?"

"He came to me Monday morning while I was handing out the daily tasks for the troops and requested to join me for training that afternoon. He then asked if I could teach him a few tricks, and then one thing led to another and now he's quite skilled with the blade. That's all I can tell you." He explained and began gathering his equipment.

I felt angry. I thought we were friends, why would he keep secrets from Layla and I? After I shared my entire world with him. Layla has been there for him whenever things got rough and this is how he treats us? The anger grew in me and I went to blast a rock that sat in the garden but I couldn't raise my arm. I looked down and realized it had been banded to my side by vines...

"You should really try to work on your temper," came a voice from the tree. I looked up and saw Serenity perched on a branch.

"Ha-ha very funny, can you let me go now?" I grunted as I struggled.

She waved her arm and the vines shrank back into the ground. "First a rock and you never know, next could be a person." She said playfully and jumped down from the tree landing right next to me. "Jack will come around eventually so don't worry."

"I know. It's just I don't really need to have to worry about something else right now. But I can't imagine what kind of stress you might be feeling." I told her.

She sighed and looked up at me. I suddenly felt nervous as her green eyes stared into my red ones. "I feel pain deep down, but that's where I like to keep it. I try to stay positive and upbeat because it's the only thing that keeps me from going insane and lashing my magic at everyone and everything."

"What do you mean? Are you saying that I should just stop feeling sad and angry?"

"No, what I'm saying is that we have to keep our emotions in check. We are the children of gods Raven. Our emotions can have dangerous effects on the powerful magic we possess. If we can't control our emotions, our magic will control us."

I didn't want to admit it, but she was right. Every time I have gotten angry, I have destroyed something. The rock, and the mural, and if I'm not careful, I couldn't hurt someone I care about. It is my responsibility to shove all those negative feelings deep down where they can't hurt me or anyone else again.

"Thanks Serenity, I really needed that."

"Silly Griffin, that's one of the many lectures you'll get while I'm around." She pushed me playfully and I dragged us both down onto the silk like grass. We both laughed and I caught myself looking into her beautiful eyes again. I tried to not make it look obvious and tried to change the topic.

"So, have you ever combined your magic with someone else before?" I said, breaking away from her eyes, looking into the stratosphere.

She had a guilty look on her face but hesitantly responded. "Not like what we're about to attempt tomorrow, but yes I have."

"When I was little, my friends and I used to play this game where we would perform our best tricks with magic. My friend Talerva could manipulate the size of objects but she was only learning how to use her magic back then. I could barely sprout a branch at that age but that's when we had the idea to combine our magic. I grew a small flower from the ground and she used her magic to make it bigger, but it didn't turn out like we expected. The flower grew and grew but it wouldn't stop growing. Talerva and I tried to stop it but my mother had to put a stop to it herself. When it stopped growing it was bigger than the twisted tree, but it was beautiful. That's when I learned that combining magic can have amazing but also dangerous effects."

When Serenity said 'dangerous' it sent shivers down my spine. If they made a flower the size of a house then I couldn't imagine what could come from two teenagers, both children of gods, channeling all their power into moving a wheel made by gods. And what if my emotions got the better of me again? What if I ended up hurting one of my friends? The friends that brought me so far and been there even though they didn't understand a bit of it. I don't think I could live with that.

"I don't think I can do it." I said worried and sat up. All the worst possibilities flew around my mind and crushed my confidence. I suddenly felt like I had no chance at success. Serenity took me under her arm and comforted me.

"Raven, you have had it worse. You lost your family and your home-"

"Wow, way to go at making me feel better!" I snapped.

"But now is your chance to change all that. Now is your chance to go back and redo it all. The chance to see your father and home again. Don't you want that?"

I got up and pondered for a moment. The gentle breeze ruffled my long hair and I stared off at the city skyline as the sun settled behind it. I knew what I had to do to get home, but the fear of failing and hurting the people I cared about stopped me from doing it. But then I realized, if I didn't, I'd be stuck here knowing I could have changed things.. I turned to Serenity and knelt down to see her smooth face waiting for a response.

"Let's turn this damn wheel"

13

AN UNEXPECTED ALLY

~~~

I felt the cool air on my face as the A.S Destiny flew across Leafstonia to the gateway. I will admit, my nerves were all over the place. With feeling the pressure of turning the wheel and opening the gateway to Atlasdam, and Jack ignoring us, I was feeling pretty stressed. Layla told me that she tried to talk to Jack but he said that there was nothing wrong. I then told Layla the conversation I overheard between him and Darius. We both wondered what had gotten into him and we both agreed that we would confront him once we got to Atlasdam, that was if me and Serenity succeed...

We arrived at the temple, and I settled the ship down inside it. I stood in the path of the gateway to Atlasdam and stared at the kingdom crest atop the door. The Griffin behind the flame that symbolized my kingdom's crest reminded me of the importance that we succeed. This was it. Atlasdam or bust. Serenity waited for me at the wheel and gave me a supporting smile.
~~~

"Whenever you're ready." she said.

I nodded and walked to the middle of the room, I looked at Jack and his head turned once he saw me look at him. I ignored it because I needed my mind clear and free of negativity. This was about to get messy...

"Ready?" I asked.

Serenity nodded

I closed my eyes, I held out my hands, and mentally prepared my body for what it was about to go through. The power within me channeled throughout my body stronger than I could ever imagine. The wheel started to glow red and that was Serenity's signal to channel her magic. She wrapped several vines around the wheel and in the mechanism itself and tried to turn the wheel. I felt pain and burning in myself as I felt the magic overcame me. Serenity screamed in frustration as we struggled with all our might, but I wasn't giving up. I channeled more of my strength and the pain got even more intense. I felt like I was in a blazing inferno, and I latched on by the chains of my emotions. The wheel wouldn't budge as we both poured our very souls out of our teenage bodies. The anger grew inside me as I felt the power grow. I started to come off the ground and my eyes shone red like stars. I let the anger through as it made me stronger, and I felt like I could do it. I could hear my friends calling out to me again, but I tuned them out. The power surrounded the wheel and cracks formed in the stone. I tried to stop it before I went any further, but I wasn't strong enough, I was too far gone. More and more cracks appeared in the wheel, and it was too late. I destroyed the wheel...

Everything stopped and I fell from the air and collapsed on the temple floor. I expected someone to come and help me, but I was wrong, all three of them were paralyzed in shock. I looked at what was left of the wheel, and I swallowed the large apple in my throat when I saw it. There was nothing left, only dust. I looked at my friends, but they didn't look back, they were white as ghosts and Layla was on her knees. I tried to get to my feet, but I stumbled back to the ground. Chip moved around in my pocket, so I lifted him out and held him in front of me. He looked dizzy but also scared, but it was nothing compared to Jack's face. His face grew red, and he looked furious.

"And the son of a god does it again!" He shouted as it echoed through the room.

"Guys I'm sorry-"

"Yeah, the all-powerful Raven couldn't turn a goddam wheel without completely destroying it!"

"Jack what are you-" Layla tried to say but Jack cut

her off.

“No Layla, I'm sick of it. I'm sick of him thinking he can do what he wants just because he has magic powers!”

“What the hell are you talking about? I have never thrown my weight around! If there's anything I'm sick of it's you ignoring us for absolutely no reason.” I argued and got to my feet as I leaned against a pillar.

“We can't even go home now. All because you couldn’t control your little temper tantrums!”

“Well excuse me for literally going through hell the past ten years. It's not exactly my fault for having my life torn apart and then having to feel the responsibility of getting everyone safely across the universe!”

“Do you really think you’re the only person in this room that has suffered Raven?! Do you really think that you’re the only person whose life was destroyed in the blink of an eye?” Jack yelled senselessly with aggression.

We all just stood and stared speechless.

“You want to know why I have been training with Darius? I have been training with Darius so I can be strong enough to get over all the trauma, so I can forget about it at the most important times.

Darius has been helping me to be stronger but not just physically."

"But Darius said that you're never weak if you have friends..." Layla chimed in

"Well, it's kind of hard to feel strong when your friend turns things to dust when he's angry." he huffed.

As those words settled in our minds, Jack stormed out of the temple and sat on a rock in the woods to process what had just happened. As for me, I didn't know what to do next. I felt like I had hit rock bottom and the ladder to climb back up had finally given away. My legs had no strength to stand and I sat down against the pillar and sobbed as the horrible feeling of failure blackened my heart. I sat there, staring at the closed door to Atlasdam realizing it would never open. The feeling of never seeing its sun rise over the gardens again was too much to handle. All was lost. The fire had gone out. But just as the ashes began to cool, I saw a spark. A blue spark, like something was turning on before me. Then more sparkles appeared and started to form a gap in space right before me. The gap opened up and revealed a man on the other side.

"It's....Its......a..... portal!" Serenity struggled to say as she started into the magic of it.

The person walked out into the temple and the

portal closed behind him. He was a grown man with long silver hair and silver eyes. He wore a short cloak that stopped at his waist and gray boots that looked like they were made for Royalty. I instantly recognized the clothing and realized that he was Atlian, one of my people...

"Raven Griffin, I am Therion Stone, and I have come to take you home." he spoke, his voice stern but caring at the same time. He sounded like he knew I was here at this exact moment.

I sprung to my feet and ran over to him. "Your T.S! The captain of the A.S Destiny! You were the one that my father trusted to find me!" I explained excitedly.

"Yes, your Highness, you must have found my Journal on the ship. We have quite a bit to discuss. Mistress Serenity, I would advise that you accompany us to Atlasdam. We may have a lead on the location of your mother." Therion told us.

Serenity breathed heavily but made to keep her composure. "How do you know me and my mother?"

"And what of my father, Therion?" I asked.

"All will be explained in due time my friends. As for now, let us return to Atlasdam. I trust you have taken care of my old friend the Destiny." He said with pride and marched out of the temple towards the ship.

What was hopelessness and despair, was replaced by excitement and overwhelming happiness. I could finally say with absolute certainty; I was going home.

We all boarded the A.S Destiny including Jack who was still sulking even though we were going home. Therion stood at the front of the ship and began moving his hands in a spell like motion. In front of the ship appeared a large portal and on the other side was the very place I hoped to see for the last 10 years. The light of the other side shone into the dim forest and into my eyes. We flew through the portal and my heart jumped out of its place when I saw the sunrise over my home.

The tall buildings casted long shadows onto the suburbs of the city as smoke rose from the chimneys of the buildings. Leafstonia and Atlasdam were very different in architecture. While Leafstonia made its buildings from more natural resources, like wood and stone, we constructed our city with less commonly known materials. Most buildings are made of a white stone we found a mass supply of. We called it Atly Quartzite as it was only ever found in our realm.

It was quite overwhelming to finally be here after all this time and my eyes started to tear up, but I saved the water works for when I see my father. But I kept wondering how Therion came to find me in the first place.

“How was it that you came to find me, Therion?” I pondered

“When your father first assigned me to the task of finding you, he gave me a unique device, crafted by engineers in the steampunk regions of our realm.” Therion pulled out a compass like device from his pocket. “It can track an individual’s magic with a strand of DNA. We extracted your DNA from your belongings and waited for it to react, but it never did. Medusa must have had a tracking cloak casted on the Underworld. But just a little while ago, the compass started going insane, the readings were off the chart and it told me all this was happening in Leafstonia.”

“It must have reacted to all the magic you used trying to turn the wheel.” Serenity added. “But you're not a god. How did you open that portal?”

“The King gave me another little trinket before I set off. A Gateway Medallion.” he said and pointed to a gold medal with a gem in the middle on his cloak. "Allows the wearer to open portals to any of the known realms.”

“So how come it didn’t go off all the other times Raven used magic?” Layla queried

“I don’t know for sure, but it could have something

to do with him discovering the Gateway Temple. That place has been told to do peculiar things to one's soul. Perhaps the evil that dwells in the underworld still lingered."

"Well, you're home now and that's all that matters." Jack said in an unwelcoming tone.

"I just can't wait to see my father. He's probably sitting on the throne waiting for me to come busting through the doors of the Palace." I exclaimed and looked at Therion but his face dropped. He looked disappointed, and almost sad. Something wasn't right. "My father is here......right Therion?" He looked away from me but I grabbed his shoulder and turned him to face me. "Therion, where is my father?" I demanded.

"I'm sorry your highness, but he has disappeared, and has been gone for months..."

14

THE PRINCE OF ATLASDAM

~~~

We settled the Destiny at the Palace airship docks and I burst through the throne room doors to see an empty throne. My worst fears were confirmed as I called out for my father and no one responded but my own voice echoing back. Therion spoke the truth, Triton was nowere to be found. My head was spinning as I continued to run around the Palace and call my father's name, my friends running after me trying to get me to stop. I tripped in the halls and looked down to see a flower had overgrown and wrapped itself around my ankle.

"Serenity let me go!" I yelled in frustration.

She knelt down and placed her hand on my face. She looked into my eyes with hers and spoke softly. "Raven, you know as well as I that there's no point in freaking out. We will find him."

Everyone was looking down at me while I pathetically panicked on the floor like a child. Therion appeared from being Serenity.
~~~

"We're all going to meet in the War room for a meeting. We have a lot to discuss." Therion explained.

Serenity released me and pulled me up. My nerves were all over the place and I didn't know what to feel anymore. Should I be happy I'm finally home? Or should I be sad that my father has gone missing? I just wanted to curl up into a little ball and disappear into the void of my insanity. Chip sensed that I was uneasy and flew onto my shoulder. He nuzzled me with his tiny head, but this time, not even Chip could keep the nightmares away. Serenity held onto my hand and whipped my tears.

"Take your time. I can't imagine what you're feeling, but I can imagine that you want to take a look around and gather yourself before we discuss the worst." She told me. I nodded in agreement. "Come to the war room when you're ready." she said and she and Therion disappeared down the hall.

I got up and gained my composure. The feeling of returning to the place you grew up in after ten years was weird. Nothing had changed. Same statues, same halls, same banners, same guards that stood there awkwardly. As I passed by, some of them looked shocked and a few looked confused. But I didn't get stopped once. It was like they already knew who I was. There were whispers and they pointed, but I didn't care. There was one place I wanted to see, and some nosey guards weren't going to stop me. I made my way to the east wing of the castle to climb the tall staircase that led to my old bedroom. The stairs were as long as I remembered, but I reached the top of the stairs and entered the room.

It hadn't changed a bit since I could remember. Same tall ceiling and big windows. My bed, messy always, and the bathroom was still bright and shiny. On the opposite side of the room was a door that led to outside. A small bridge connected my room to a tower and that's where my playroom was. I opened the door to the playroom and I was instantly overwhelmed with memories. The table my friends and I always turned into a fort and the long leather sofa we had countless naps on. Flashbacks sparkled in my eyes and I could see my friends and I running round the room. The laughter and cheers of my childhood danced round my mind as I was reminded of the great times I had. I sat on the window sill and looked out onto my beloved kingdom. The view was always breathtaking from my playroom. You could see the entire city like you have seen it for the first time. Airships passed by and the sun was just setting, casting a beautiful pink light onto the tall buildings. As I gazed upon my realm, I realized that I needed to see the place I loved more than any other in the entire Universe. The window slid open and I flew out down to the courtyard.

At the end of the courtyard stood a hedge arch that led into the place I wanted to be in for a long time. The place I've had picnics and watched ships fly by for hours. The Royal gardens of Atlasdam. I passed the archway and happy tears rolled down my face, but I didn't stop them. My heart needed me to walk through the garden, and it was as beautiful as ever. The flowers, the bushes, and the fountain I used to splash in and get in trouble for. I sat at the fountain and took a deep breath. The sense of safety and tranquility filled my body, and I relaxed. I felt like a child again. I felt like I was waiting for my mother to bring out her baked goods, but I knew she wasn't. Rhea was the only one that made the gardens what they were, and unfortunately, they will never be the same again. I got up and wandered for a bit but I came across something I hadn't seen in the gardens before. Behind the fountain, was a statue of my mother and I. It was me as a child and my mother was holding my hand. The stone statues were so life-like. It was like my actual mother was before me. On the statue's platform, there was a silver plate with words engraved into it.

"For our beloved Queen and Prince, may they one day return to us safely"

The people made this for us, hoping that we would return. Well at least one of us did. I still wish that I could have saved her. How am I going to tell everyone that I killed my own mother? How will everyone react? That's when I knew it was time. Time to face the music.

I flew back to the Palace and stood at the double doors of the war room. I was about to swing them open but a voice said my name. I turned around and a girl with blonde hair in a long white and gold coat stood before me. She held a long golden staff with a shiny blue gem.

"Raven, is it really you?" The girl said. She looked young, maybe 16 or 17. She looked shocked to see me but she seemed familiar to me. Her eyes connected with mine and with that single connection, I knew who she was.

"It's nice to see you again, Ophilia Walker." I said and opened my arms. She jumped into them and squeezed the life out of me. To see one of my best friends after so long was a feeling I couldn't describe as I felt the warmth of her embrace. She pulled away from me and the happy disbelief was all over her face.

"When Therion said that you had returned, I had to see it with my own eyes. What happened? Did you find Triton?" Ophilia asked.

I held her hands and shook them gently. "I understand you have many questions, but I will explain everything inside. But where's Alyfn?" I responded.

She grinned. "Still the boy from the garden I see. Open the doors and find out."

I turned around and swung open the doors of the war room. Everyone had gathered around a long glass table. Sitting in a seat at the front of the table was a boy I was very familiar with. The knight in shining Armor in all our games, Alfyn St. Pine.

"Welcome your highness" He said jokingly

"At ease, soldier." I saluted.

I hugged him and felt him slightly shaking in my arms, but I could tell he didn't want me to know that. He pulled away and my eyes bounced up and down, and I had to admit that I was impressed. He had shaved the sides of his hair and the rest tied in a knot at the back. He wore the dark green garbs of the royal guard and had an Atlian sword on his hip. He wore the dark green garbs of the royal guard and had an Atlian sword belted on his hip. It seemed like he pursued his dream of being a knight. Ophilia looked like she was taking after her mother in taking up sorcery. I turned around to see her but she vanished, but I turned back to the table to see her sitting next to Layla.

"Teleportation spell." She said and winked.

I was really happy that both my friends were doing

well, but manners had to be taken care of, then we could all catch up. I marched to the top of the war table and sat down in the large chair that my father once used to sit in. All eyes in the room were on me and I suddenly felt nervous, wanting to sink into the chair even deeper. But the Prince of Atlasdam had returned. And as the prince I had to take action when needed. I held my head high and spoke.

"Now I know you all have many questions, but let me first fill you in on everything that has happened the moment I disappeared." I explained.

My story began when Medusa had dragged me into the underworld and what I figured out while I made my escape. When I landed on earth and met Charissa and discovered the library under the house. And the 'prophecy' I happened to discover in a book.

"A boy of Revenge and Love?" Alfyn asked and pondered to himself for a moment.

"Yes, I discovered that text while I was on my travels searching for the young prince. I believe that it refers to Raven himself." Therion explained while standing behind me.

I was confused by this statement. "Me, how could it refer to me?"

Serenity chimed in. "Your father is Triton, God of Revenge. And your mother is Rhea, Goddess of love."

"Exactly Princess. I believe that his highness is destined to prevent the thing I believe is coming."

I was quite lost. "What do you mean Therion? Something is coming?"

"Gods don't just disappear overnight, Ray." said Ophilia. "Fertility, Triton and you said Hermes was nowhere to be found in the temple."

"And we have had contact by the other realms, reporting that their gods have also gone missing. These things add up." Alfyn added.

"What about that compass thingy you used to find Raven." Layla asked. "Can't you track Triton or Fertility with it?"

Therion pulled out his compass again and showed it to us, the dial still sensing my presence as it fidgeted beneath the glass. "I did attempt myself the day after his majesty went missing. But I'm afraid that I haven't gotten a strong enough reading to pinpoint a location."

"So, we wait for a stronger reading. Wherever these gods are, they have to use their almighty powers at one point or another." Jack mentioned.

"We can't wait around for something to happen!" I pipped and clenched my fist aggravation. "My father spent eight years looking for me. He didn't want to stop. But when he gave up, I can imagine he was utterly and devastatingly gut wrenched. So, if you think that I am going to sit around and wait for this little thing to start buzzing, then think again. I will not rest until we scour every corner of every realm, and the Gods are found."

The deafening silence in the room felt hard after I spoke. Jack had his head down and guilt painted on his face.

"Well said your highness." Therion commended.

"So, what are you going to do?" Layla asked with bright eyes.

I had an idea, but I was going to need help. "Therion, do you still know those inventors in the steampunk region?" I asked and turned to him.

"Of course, why do you ask?"

"Send them a message, we need to have a big order."

15

A TOWN IN THE CLOUDS

~~~

I told everyone my idea for how we could locate the gods and why we would need the Steampunks. The inventors in the north region in a town called Coldera, invented the device that reacted to my power signature. According to Therion, Hendrick Hastings is the mayor of this town, and he was the one that invented the little tracking compass. But that was ten years ago. Surely, he has invented more advanced trinkets and other magic technology. Therion alerted Hastings of my arrival and that we wouldn't be leaving empty handed. Alfyn warned me to be careful what I say around these people as they are offended easily, but I took no notice of it. I dressed myself formally for this meeting in my royal black robe. Its nick piece stood tall and was stitched with fur that glided across the back of my head. It was cozy and far more comfortable than a cheap hoodie or those rags we made from turnup bags.

Alfyn and Therion were familiar with Coldera so they accompanied me as we made the journey.
~~~

Therion had control of the Destiny as he knew exactly where he was going. As for me, I was trying to handle the breathtaking view from this height. I have only ever seen the Capital city of Atlasdam. My eyes couldn't believe seeing all this for the first time. The long sparkling waterfalls pouring from the titanic mountain peaks and crashing onto crystal clear lagoons.

The flocks of winged horses majestically gliding through clouds, carrying their young on their backs. One flew right next to the Destiny and towards me. It came closer and the beautiful creature let me stroke its mane. The golden white mane felt like running my fingers through a cloud. Light, soft, and full of life. The Pegasus neighed at me and flew back to its flock. The smile kept spreading across my face as I saw even the animals of this world enjoy their lives with their families. Something I hadn't felt in a long time.

"Wait until I show you the stables back at the palace." Alfyn said, jumping down from the support beam of the mast. "The knights ride pegasi when they do their patrol around the city. Maybe they will even let you ride one."

"I mean I can already fly. But the feeling of flying as one, man and horse, would feel better than flying on my own." Chip got restless in my pocket. I peeked into my pocket and saw him looking at me angrily. "Don't worry bud,' you'll always fly with me." He whistled a tune of satisfaction and retreated to the comfort of my robe pocket.

"Keep an eye out you two, were almost at Coldera." Therion announced from the top deck.

I moved to the front of the ship and looked to the ground for a settlement. But all I could see were mountains connecting where they met. I looked to Alfyn to see where he was looking and his gaze was set straight into the sea of clouds. I looked in his direction and the clouds slowly revealed land, but not on the ground. The 'land' was airborne. The entire town was in the sky. As we got closer, I noticed humongous machines underneath the floating earth. They were mighty well-built turbines rotating faster than the eye could process. They were what was keeping the groups of land in the air. On the islands was the town of Coldera. Buildings made of brass, copper, and other variants of metals, stood together in random bunches on the islands. In the center of it all was a tall tower with a bright light emanating from the tip of the spire. It was as bright as a star and sparked like electricity every so often. I didn't know what it was but something told me that I was going to find out.

We pulled into the Airship Port of the town and we were the center of attention for everyone there. We caught the faint sound of whisperings as we walked by, daggers being shot in our direction.

"So much for the welcoming committee" I remarked.

"That's expected when you arrive in a district that doesn't use magic." Alfyn added and wrapped himself in his coat to be discreet.

I was thrown in disbelief by this. A city in the sky, in a realm full of cosmic and mystical wonders, and not using it? How do they live? How do they generate the power to lift entire islands from the ground and build a whole town upon it?

"Most citizens in Coldera are without magical abilities." Therion elucidated.

"When Hastings was born in the capital as a mere mortal, he wasn't very pleased when he realized he would never have magic in his blood. But I have to admit that he became very skilled in the arts of inventing. That's when he applied that skill into starting Coldera. Much like how your father did, Hastings invited people like him to come and join his small town, people that weren't born with magical abilities. But unfortunately, he spread lies about us magic folk, that we were hoarding all the power for ourselves."

"But that's completely untrue. Magic runs through the very air of our realm. Couldn't they harness that somehow?" I suggested.

"That's what Hastings is doing." Alfyn said." You

saw that spire when we flew in. That's drawing magic from the very life blood of our realm and converting it into power. That's how this place stays in the sky."

I was disgusted. My father founded this realm for people to live free and happy. For people all over the Universe to come and start anew. And then Hastings leaves and spreads lies and deceit about us magic users. The icky feeling in my stomach suddenly made me not want to engage in this transaction. I didn't want anything to do with this envious snake.

"Let's just go back to the ship." I said and turned around

Alfyn grabbed my robe hood and dragged me back. "You want to find Triton, right? "He asked and I nodded. "Well even though Hastings might be a prick, he's the only one that can make something strong enough to find your dad."

"I must concur with Alfyn your highness. Although he may be deceitful, Hastings has been known to provide quality material when given the right payment. The only thing he desires more than lies, is money."

As much as I wanted to turn back and head back to the city, I had to do what was best for my people. Get the machine and find my father.

"Fine, but don't hold me back if things get heated." I sarcastically requested.

Therion told us that Hastings was waiting for us in town hall and that we were headed there. We continued along the road, the poorly paved brick road to the Town hall and arrived at what seemed to be the square. In the middle of it was the spire and it was even brighter up close. The power radiating from it pinched my brain as I felt its strength. I had never felt this much concentrated magic before. It made me feel abhorrent to be near such a device. But that's how these people need to live.

Many people stood gawking at us as we inspected the spire. A man had the audacity to approach us and started giving us hell but we paid no attention to him.

"Go back to yer' fancy city ye' bunch of bloody royals!" He provoked, but we said nothing and walked away.

He grabbed my shoulder and I casted a mild shock to his hand.

"Ow! Oh, ye'll pay for that..."

He clenched his fist and went to strike the back of my head, but Alfyn caught it and used his body weight against him to swing him round and crash him to the ground. He stepped away from his crippled victim and looked at him pitifully.

"Didn't see me using magic there now did you?" He smirked.

The man quickly got to his feet and cowardly dashed down an alleyway. Everyone who witnessed it lowered their heads and didn't dare glance at us again. We trekked up the hill to town hall and got stopped by a pair of guards.

"And what do you think you're doing? Walking up here like you own the place." The guard goaded.

"We have business with Hendrick Hastings, and we aren't really in the mood for the delays" I countered.

"Oh wait, this is the prince whose dad abandoned him!" The other guard mocked.

I dug my fingernails into my palms and nearly popped a blood vessel trying to hold back the urge to turn this low life inside out and show everyone how ugly he was on the inside. But I shoved past the dying hyenas and marched into the building head on. If Hastings was as pigheaded as his 'people' then we were going to have some issues. Some less discourteous individuals pointed us in the direction of Hastings's office and they directed us to a large staircase. At the top we were met by a fancy copper door with the letters 'HH' on a plaque bolted to the front. Before I knocked on the door, I looked at Therion and Alfyn and they didn't look any more eager than I was, which I wasn't. Not one bit

"Just stay cool." Alfyn said and patted me on the shoulder for support, because I could tell that he knew I was going to need it.

I knocked, the door opened and we were greeted by a woman in a short brown dress with her legs in knee-high boots made out of bronze.

"Ah, Master Griffin and company, please come in." She greeted us warmly and closed the door behind us.

The office was grand but wasn't very office-like. Everything was made out of either bronze or copper so the colors weren't very vibrant. Everything was bolted to the wall and held firmly with metal frames. In the middle of the room before a tall window stood a long desk, also made of bronze and copper. This guy really didn't have any taste for décor. In the far corner of the room was a miniature playset. I looked closer and it was a small-scale depiction of Coldera. There were even tiny working turbines holding up the model islands.

"Was the first ever model!", came a voice.

I looked in its direction and a large leather chair spun round from behind the desk, revealing a rotund middle-aged man. He was wearing a brown jacket that didn't go all the way round his body and a long top hat with mechanic goggles strapped around sat on his bald head. His thin line of hair went round his head and matched his small stuffy moustache. He wore an advanced looking monocle on his left eye that looked like it was ticking like a clock. Small gears clicked together on the glass, as though it was calculating something.

"Ye' must be Raven. I av' heard all abou' you..." he stated roughly. His accent was thick and similar to the goblins in the underworld, making me instantly dislike it.

"And you must be Hastings. I must say it's quite a town you have here. I'm particularly impressed by how you keep the town aloft." I complimented it through my grinding teeth.

"Well tank' ye very much. It was easy really. I built a machine tha' digs straight into the ground an' implants the turbines so the land can rise straight into the air. Thought it would add a bit of flare yeno'." He boasted. I was sick of this already.

"Hastings, we were hoping you could build us a machine that can help us track down Triton and the other gods." Therion said. He pulled out the magic tracking compass from his pocket and showed it to Hastings. "Like this, but capable of tracking with a weaker power signature."

“And why would I do tha’.” He snickered and grinned, leaning back in his chair, kicking his feet onto the table.

Alfyn reached into his bag and pulled out a smaller one. He dumped it onto the desk and the bag opened, showing the greedy man a large sum of gold. Hastings laughed and leaned back in his chair.

“Tha’ aint gonna’ work a second time.” He smirked.

Alfyn slammed his hands down on the desk and looked Hastings dead in the eyes.

“Listen bud, you'll make this damn machine, or I’ll kick that bag of gold right up your-”

“Alfyn, that's enough.” Therion interrupted. “Hastings. Triton himself will commend you with far more if you help us find him. Build us the machine...and you will be known as a hero throughout the realm. Our kinds may not get along, but that doesn’t have to stop you from doing the right thing.” He monotoned as Hastings struggled to stop himself from laughing.

He fell back in his chair like a child dying of laughter.

“Ye probably tink’ I will just change my mind after tha’ lil’ speech of yers.’ But guess wha’. I ain't doing it. You tink’ that yer’ better than me cus’ ye can lift rocks and fly? I built this ere' place fer' people like me. Fer' people tha' get the same abuse tha' I got fer' not being able to do anytin' special. An then you lot come marching demanding I build this ere' machine. Ha! I don' tink' so." He denounced.

I didn't know this man had it hard. I thought he was just jealous of not having magic in his blood, but it was really just because of the oppression of being no magic. I guess he just wanted to give people like him a place to be themselves without feeling pressured to be something they aren't. Maybe the lies and rumors were just stereotypes for the people in this town and they too have been oppressed. But then again, I only knew the man for five minutes. Actions speak louder than words.

"Hastings, I'm sorry for whatever happened to you in the past." I enunciated "But someone once told me that the past is something we cannot change. But the future is what we make it. You have the chance to prove to everyone that ever doubted you. The chance to prove you deserve to be a part of this realm by showing them your capability even without being able to lift rocks and potentially crushing them in the process. So please, help us find my father, and no one will ever doubt non-magic folk ever again. That I promise."

Hastings sighed and adjusted his monocle. He looked defeated by my words. His face told us that he knew what he was going to do.

"Lord, ye' really are a bunch of saps." He grunted "Fine, but only to clean the name of me people..."

16

A GODLY INVENTION

~~~

Hastings began work on the machine right away and we all contributed to helping him. I used my magic to lift supplies to the workshop and hold things together. Therion and Jack did some other heavy lifting but it made me wonder something. What were their powers? I have never heard them talk about them before, and it made me want to ask them. I approached Jack during a break session and asked him about it.

"Well, I haven't really 'unlocked' my powers yet." He said, slightly embarrassed.

"What kind of powers are they? And 'unlocked'?" I asked.

"Well, the entire Pine family tree has been known to be shapeshifters. The ability to transform into any animal we have seen with our own eyes. We've also been known to unlock our magic at a very late age. My dad only unlocked his when he was eighteen."
~~~

“So, when do you think you will be able to unlock yours?” I asked.

“No clue. It could be right now, or ten years from now.” He stated. “But it will happen, gut feeling you know? Now as for Therion, he does have magic but he doesn’t like talking about it, let alone even using it.”

“So have you ever seen Therion using his magic?”

“No, he’s a walking enigma. No one knows anything about him except for your dad, he must have trusted him for a reason.” He vacillated.

Alfyn was right. I didn't know much about Therion, but my father trusted him to search the universe for me. And he went out of his way to come to the gateway temple to find me. He brought us to Hastings to build the machine so we could find my father. There wasn’t a reason I shouldn’t trust him. But it did make me wonder why my father trusted him so much. And why Therion is so loyal to my father. But all that was going to have to wait. Our main priority was building this machine.

Hastings had many people working for him so we made good progress on the machine. Hastings planned to connect it to the town's spire to power it because he said it was going to need a lot of juice. But he told us that the machine alone wouldn’t track the gods. We needed a DNA strand from every god that we needed to find. I contacted Ophilia and asked for her help.

"You have got to be kidding me." She complained.

Before we left for Coldera, Ophilia taught me a spell so I could contact people through an astral projection. It was like a video call on a cell phone but with magic. I could see her on the other side of the red aura floating in my hand and she didn't look very happy. Then again, I was asking her to collect a DNA strand of every god that had gone missing, and we're talking quite a few. We had many people contact us, informing us that their rulers had gone missing. This was happening all across the universe and everyone was getting worried. We all thought that this was a harbinger in disguise, warning us about something much bigger. But this machine would stop all that if we had the right ingredients.

"Come Ophilia you have to. Use Therion's medallion and take the Destiny." I offered.

"Raven, do you have any idea how tedious that will be? We're talking 10 realms, maybe even 15. And people don't always take kindly to random folk waltzing and searching their God's shower drains for strands of hair." She gagged at the mention of it.

"I know it's a big ask but the fate of the Gods rests on this. It's the one thing to get this stupid thing to work! Start with my fathers, that can't be that hard right?" I tried to make things light.

She wasn't amused. "Fine but it will take me a while. Serenity and Layla said they would come with me. I'm quite fond of those two. But that Jack guy rubbed me the wrong way."

"I know. He's been a bit of a pain recently but don't let that stop you. He'll come around at some point." I told her.

"Let's hope. I'll let you know when we've collected the DNA. And have that machine done by the time we're back." she said and disappeared from view.

We continued to build the machine and it gave me a chance to get to know Hastings better, not that I particularly wanted to. He was very full of himself and always wanted to talk about was how great he was. The universal inventions he has created and his 'impact' on technological advancement in Atlasdam. I despised everything that escaped his lips but Alfyn told me to just endure it for now. Even Chip was looking at me weird when Hastings had a rant. But there was one thing I wanted to know about him. Me and him were alone while melding metal to the machine, that's when I asked him.

"Hasting can I ask you something?" I asked but something told me I would soon regret it.

"Wot' is it?" He grunted and examined the machines blue print.

"What exactly happened to you to make you want to start Coldera, if you don't mind me asking."

He looked up at me sternly and sighed. His monocle ticked in the silence and he took his hat from his head.

"Six years went by an' I never go' a sign of magic inside me." He began and removed his monocle. "Ma' whole family had magic in them an' I was hated to bits fer' no' being 'special'. The kids on the street would hang me in trees an' pu' curses on me fer' no' having any magic. I wos' yer' age and even my own parents didn't like me. So, they kicked me to the gee'. I was livin' on scraps fer' months and was all alone. But then an old scraper found me and said I could work fer em' in exchange for a place to live. I'd work on airships an' other things, bu' I wasn't any appier' than I was a' home. The man roared a' me whenever I screwed up and give me a clap wi' the back of is' and'. But one day I started fiddling wi' little gismos on ships. I'd make small things like tiny planes and walking robots. Someone spotted me talent and gave me an' opportunity to work in the fancy parts of the Capital."

"I learned how to tinker wit' tings' way better and became one of der' best workers. That place wos' great an all but I felt like I was being watched the whole time. Whenever I made somethin' new, me coworkers would give me dirty looks an' whisper. One day after a long day working on a big project of mine, I fell asleep at my desk. But I was tick' enough to leave my project plans on me' desk. The project I wos' working on' wos' a brand-new model of bionic limbs. I thought it would really help some people, but I got duped. When it came time to show the boss me' idea, I got fired. Apparently one of my coworkers already turned in tha' exact same idea. The bastard stole me work, and of course he was a magic user. I tried to convince the boss it was my idea first. But he thought I was a piece of filth for copying someone jus' because I didn't have magic. I wos' alone again"

"So, when did you start Coldera?" I asked.

"I continued me' work alone and showed no one a thing' cus' I learned that people will steal the eye ou' of yer' socket. Then I decided to work on the turbine. The very turbine tha' holds up the land ye' walk on. After many failed prototypes I finally go' the working, but I need somethin' to power a machine tha' strong. Then I started workin' on the spire. It draws magic from the very air and converts it into energy to power the town. Just like yer' dad, I invited people from all over to come and live in my small town. It started off with one island then it turned into the nation you now see."

I had no idea people from Atlasdam could be so

cruel. Now I understand why Hastings hates us magic people. He had no one there for him for years, something I could relate to on many levels. Then when he thought he found his place, he was betrayed by his coworkers. The man had it very hard. He built this place to give people like him somewhere to live without hate and despair. I admired that about him. It reminded me of my father, luckily it was the only thing he reminded me of. He has a passion for his people and his work, and that deserves an ocean of respect.

"I'm sorry you had to go through that" I gave my condolence

"Spare me the pity, I've heard it all before." He barked and aggressively put his hat back on his bald head while walking away. That went well...

One night after a day of building, I decided to explore the city a bit. I chose flight over walking through the town as I was not in the mood for the unpleasant townsfolk. I flew around and admired the cool inventions dotted around the town. My eyes caught a glimpse of a contraption that glided across farms and harvested crops as it went. By the docks I saw a merchant dealing weapons to soldiers and they were very advanced looking. One man held a shield that could retract into a small trinket in an instant. Another man was carrying a bow and when he swung it, the bow folded itself so small that he could fit it in his pocket. I'd imagine Alfyn would dream that this kind of weaponry was in the armory back home. He is very flexible when it comes to the weapons in his arsenal. I was watching him train the other day and he really became the knight me and Ophilia knew he would become. He was besting even adults in combat and never missed a shot with his bow. I don't see a reason for him to be worried about having magic, he has all he needs.

I flew below the town to see the turbines holding them up and I was truly astonished how something like this was physically possible without the power of gods. Whole chunks of land being held in the sky by mere fans. All day, all night, for the past fifty years according to Therion. Hastings's talent was beyond anything I put into words, but I felt like the oppression on non-magic users was holding him back and he was an inch away from greatness. But there was nothing I could do about that now. When we find my father and bring him back, we can make a difference in society in Atlasdam, and magic and non-magic people can coexist in harmony. No one should be put down for what they can and cannot do. I knew Atlasdam as a place where people could live in peace, under a king that devoted all his time and effort to his people. I will make Atlasdam the realm my father always wanted it to be.

It took us about two weeks to finally complete the god tracking machine, but after a lot of time and talkative torture, we had a 'masterpiece'. Hastings words not mine. The machine was large and made of bronze and copper. It had two large metal poles with gems at the end of them sticking out either side of it. Therion told me that the gems were very important and that only a few remained in Atlasdam. They were called Soul crystals, and they were required to strengthen even the weakest energy signal so we could pinpoint its location. Around the machine there were small containment units where we would place the DNA strands of every god we wanted to track. On the front there was a glass screen where we would show the realm the gods were located. All we needed to do to make it work was the DNA strands and to hook it up the spire to power it.

Ophilia arrived shortly after the machine's completion. She and Serenity wheeled a large wagon off the Destiny filled glass jars. For a second, I had no idea what they could be, but when I saw what was inside them, I knew. The jars glowed with different colored lights as the wavy multicolored strands floated inside them. They were thin constructs of aura and magic that contained the DNA of the gods.

"You have no idea what we had to go through to get some of these" Serenity sighed and ran over to hug me.

I felt happy to see Serenity, and I think she was happy to see me too. I didn't know what I felt for

Serenity yet, but I knew it was more than friends. It was the way she made me feel whenever she looked at me with her stunning green eyes that made my heart skyrocket. Maybe it was the mutual determination to find our parents, but I felt a slight connection.

“A little help here” Ophilia called out, struggling to pull the wagon from the ship. Alfyn ran over and gave her a hand.

“There sure are a lot of them.” Alfyn said, pulling the wagon with Ophilia.

“It was an absolute nightmare to get them.” She complained. “We got Triton and Fertility’s first, they were easy, but after that, it all went downhill.”

“As much as I want to hear it, we don’t have time.” I noted. “We need to get this thing hooked up.” But something was missing. I looked around but it was only Ophilia and Serenity. “Where's Jack and Layla? “

Serenity gave me a disappointed look. “Jack wasn’t feeling well and Layla is looking after him back at the palace. He didn’t look the best.”

“Did you get a Doctor?” I asked.

“She’s there with him as we speak.” Ophilia added. “Layla says she’s really sorry she couldn’t make it but she wishes us the best of luck.”

I was disappointed that Layla and Jack couldn't make it. They were the ones that were with me since the beginning, but we didn't have time to get emotional about who was or wasn't here. We needed to fire up this machine.

"Let's get it started, shall we ladies?"

17

FEARFUL MEMORIES

~~~

With the machine completed, the DNA strands and the spire to power it, we had all we needed to find my father and the other gods. The hairs on my necks and arms were standing up as my nerves were bouncing all over the place. Everyone gathered in the warehouse to get this thing finally up and running, but I wanted to know one thing first.

"Which one is my fathers?" I asked Ophilia. She pointed to a jar that contained a bright red strand of glowing aura. I lifted it up and the strand touched my hand on the other side of the glass. I got a slight sensation in my fingers; it was like the aura knew. "Don't worry father, we're almost there..."

Hastings came over and pushed me aside to examine the DNA strands for himself. "So, these swirly doo daas are the DNA of the gods?" He scoffed, recklessly fiddling with one of the jars

"Yes, and if you drop that jar the strand will vanish into thin air." Ophilia snarled and carefully removed the jar from Hastings's hands.
~~~

"Oi, she a fiery one aint' she?" He mocked and scowled at Ophilia

"Why you big-"

"Give it a rest, the two of you." Serenity butted in. "We can hate each other all we want after we bring back the gods."

"Mistress Serenity is right." Therion chimed in. "Squabbling over our differences won't do us any good. Shall we start up the machine?"

Hastings broke away from his scowl. "Certainly. All ye' need to do is put them jars into those units."

Ophilia smirked at Hastings one last time and then closed her hands. She twisted her left hand and opened both wide, her staff magically appearing in front of her. She grabbed it and waved it over the jars. A blue aura surrounded them and levitated into the air. She pointed her staff at the machine and one by one the jars placed themselves into their respective spaces. Ophilia winked at me and then grinned at Hastings. His monocle ticked in sync with his eye twitch

Hastings reached into his pocket and pulled out a remote. He pointed it to a large metal container in the corner of the room and clicked a button. The container opened itself up to reveal a robust humanoid machine. It was a robot. Its arms were long and made of a thick metal. Its head was small, with only eyes to see that lit up orange. It sprung to life and moved its long legs stomped towards the large connector that was attached to the spire in the center of town. The mechanical creature lifted the connector and plugged it into the god tracker. Hastings smirked at Ophilia thinking he bested her. Ophilia went to cast a spell but I held her hand down and shook my head at her. She was above such immature behavior.

"Ye' ready for this?" Hastings said eagerly.

I looked at everyone and they looked back at me with the same look. This was it. But was I ready to know? I had no idea myself, but there was only one way to find out. I nodded at Hastings and he pointed the remote at the machine and clicked a button. The machine slowly activated, fizzing sounds from pipes and the sound of magic whirring around the place. It sounded like dust flying around and you could hear it ten times louder. The gems glowed and the magic aura in the jars soon followed. The strands of aura swirled and spun in the jars as they glowed like stars. The machine looked as though it was scanning the DNA and processing it, but something wasn't right.

The machine began shaking violently and the fizzing became painful to the ear as we all covered ours. It couldn't handle this much power. I looked outside and I was blinded by the spire as it shone brighter than the sun. Screws and bolts started shooting out from the machine leaving spouts of hot steam trying to escape. I looked at Hastings and his face grew worried as his creation came apart. But suddenly the screen on the device began to flicker. We all cautiously stared at the screen as letters revealed the realm, we all wanted to know the name off.

A-L-T-H-E-A

I had no recollection of this realm, but I didn't want to sit and figure it out, the machine was about to blow. Me and Ophilia both looked at each other and we knew what to do. I waved my wands and she waved her staff as we casted a shield around everyone in the workshop. A blue and red magic surrounded us as the machine finished giving away and exploded to pieces.

The dust settled and Ophilia and I took down the shield. All that remained was the floating strands of aura, but they too soon vanished into thin air. The explosion left a deep black crater in the middle of the workshop, Hastings on his knees as he stared into it. He started weeping like a child and held a piece of the metal that was left of the machine. The rest of us shared a look and I knew we were all thinking the same thing. Alfyn went over to him and guided him to a seat before 'assuring' him that things will be ok. As Hastings wept in the corner of the room, the rest of us inspected the crater.

"After all that work, the stupid thing ends up blowing up!" Alfyn exclaimed.

"Don't forget the fact that Serenity spent about two weeks gathering all that DNA." Ophilia added.

"Are we all just going to ignore the titan in the room?" I butted in. "Where in the universe is Althea?"

Everyone looked at me in disbelief at my words. I looked at them equally confused. "Why are you all looking at me like that?" I asked.

"Raven, do you really not know?" Ophilia said, looking at me worried.

"What are you talking about?"

"Your majesty, Althea is your mother's realm..." Therion said.

My mother's realm? The realm my she and father were at war over? The realm the two met and my mother reformed the cursed heart of my father? I didn't know how to feel about all this. Should I be happy that I finally get to see where my mother grew up? Or should I be worried that I have to be reminded that I killed my own mother corrupted by darkness? My mother never talked to me about her home when I was a child. Maybe I was too young and wouldn't understand, or maybe she was ashamed of abandoning her realm, I didn't know what to make of all of it.

"Who rules Althea now?" I asked.

"No one knows. Your grandmother-"

"I have a grandmother!?" I cut Therion off.

"You really don't know at all do you?" Alfyn asked, concerned.

The confusion overwhelmed me and I stormed off out of the workshop. The night brought a chill so I wrapped myself in my warm robe and wandered through the town. My life was a blur, I felt like I didn't know anything. Everything fell apart ten years ago and I have missed so much. I didn't even know about my mother's realm. The person I loved more than anything in this universe and I had no knowledge of the world she grew up in. What has befallen Althea now? Why are my father and the gods even there? What happened to the universe while I slaved in those mines for ten years? There was only one person that could tell everything I wanted to know, and he was in my mother's realm. Chip pecked at my ear as he sat on my shoulder. I turned my head and looked at him and looked back at me with his black pearl eyes. You know for a bird that didn't speak he was awfully persuasive. I marched back up to the workshop and swung the doors open with my magic, everyone stared at me once again, but this time I knew what to say.

"Pack up, we're heading back to Atlasdam, and then we're setting off to Althea." I announced.

We all gathered our things and made our way back to the airship port. As we walked through the town, we heard someone call out. I thought it was another magic hater, but it wasn't. It was Hastings and he was walking towards us.

"Listen kid." He began slightly out of breath from having to walk that far." I may no' ge' all this magic rubbish. Bu' ye' have guts. Go make tings' right." He said and patted me on the shoulder.

"Though our people may not get along Hastings, I am grateful for all you have done for us. I'll make sure to mention you to my father." I told him and smiled.

"Tha' is the nicest thin' any magic folk as' ever said to me..." He said and grinned.

We shook hands and said our goodbyes before he started sobbing again. I felt as though I made a difference in the feud between magic and non-magic users. The rest of us packed our things onto the Destiny and took to the skies, to Atlasdam. I looked back on Coldera and gazed upon the small but breath-taking civilization. I was still amazed how a man without powers was able to build a home for so many people from the ground up, literally. He may be a bit ignorant but his talents for inventing are unparalleled. I hoped to see the town again, but let's hope the people are more welcoming than before.

We sailed through the skies with the fresh cold air tickling our noses. I couldn't wait to tell Jack and Layla the news. Good or bad, I couldn't tell. I was still figuring out whether I should be excited or nervous about the whole thing. But above all I was truly ecstatic to see my father after ten years of cruelty. I was going to feel his arms around me again, to hear his jolly laugh again. That feeling was the best thing I have felt in a decade. It made my heart leap with joy but also relief because I didn't have to worry about where he was anymore. Happy tears rolled down my cheeks and Serenity witnessed each one, but I didn't care, I felt comfortable around her.

She came over to me and whipped my cheek with her soft hands. She gazed at me with her emerald eyes and smiled with a sparkling smile. My heart fluttered whenever I was around her and I couldn't help but feel warm inside. She never escaped my thoughts and even when I couldn't see her, I could remember every detail of her beautiful face. I smiled as I felt her cold hands on my puffy red face.

"I know how it feels." She said to me,

I was taken back by this. Did she feel the same way?

"We are about to see our parents again. That feeling of seeing them again that comes from your heart, you know?" she said sweetly.

The disappointment hit me but that didn't mean she doesn't feel the same way. But it was nice knowing I wasn't the only person that felt this way about seeing my father. But I suddenly realized a horrible truth I would eventually have to face. My father would want to know what happened to my mother. How was I going to tell him her death was my fault? I was the one that blasted the underworld ceiling and caused the earth to kill her. The guilt was too much to tell my father.

"How am I going to tell him, Serenity?" I asked worriedly.

She saw how distressed I was and looked at me with a comforting gaze. She wrapped her arms over my shoulder and spoke softly into my ear.

"He will understand. He's your father. He loves you and won't any less when he realizes there was nothing else you couldn't have done." She conceded.

"But what if-" I said but she broke away from the hug and pressed her finger on my lips, silencing me.

"He will understand, so stop worrying." She told me seriously.

I smiled and looked at her. "Alright my lady." I said sarcastically.

She pushed me playfully and we both laughed. Just then I heard someone call my name. I looked up and saw Therion looking down from the top deck. He indicated me to come. I walked up to him but he was looking straight ahead steering the ship.

"How does it feel to have the Destiny in your possession again?" I bantered.

"Well, it isn't really mine anymore, is it?" He said, still looking straight. "You were the one that brought it back to life after the awful state it was in. You poured ounces of our magic into this aircraft so it would take to the skies once more. So, if I'm not mistaken, that makes you the captain of the A.S Destiny." He said and looked at me assertively.

"Thank you." I was proud to get the respect of Therion. There was something about him that made you want to impress him. Maybe that's one of the many reasons my father trusted him.

I began to walk away but he had more to say. "That isn't actually why I wanted to speak with you, your majesty."

"Well, what's on your mind?"

"It's actually what has been on your mind lately. I couldn't help but notice that you were curious about my magic a little while ago." He explained

"Who told you that?" I asked confused.

"That actually brings me onto what I wanted to tell you. You see, your father trusted me to look for you because of the special magic that lives inside of me."

"And what is that exactly?"

"I have the unique ability to manipulate the minds of others. I can read minds. Cause others to feel excruciating pain on my command. Stop others from doing certain actions and much more. It's a very scary but dangerous magic that I have mastered over many years." Therion said looking slightly ashamed.

"That's why you don't tell many people."

"Correct your majesty. Your father knew it would be a great asset to finding you. Knowing when people are lying and knowing if someone knew your location."

"Well, if my father trusted you, I don't see a reason why I shouldn't," I told him and patted his shoulder in support.

"I see a lot of your father in you. The bravery, the admiration for others, reminds me very much of the great king." He condoled.

I really admired Therion for everything he has done for my family and Atlasdam. He searched for me for years. He watched over my home while my father was missing and continues to watch over me to this day. He was a very loyal individual, that is something that should never be overlooked in someone.

We began descending into the city and the silver moon glistened onto the shiny buildings. The city was beautiful no matter the time of day; it was one of the many reasons I love it. We landed in the courtyard and we saw Layla running down towards us. I was happy to see her but she looked even happier, almost relieved. I floated down from the ship to see her but she jumped onto me and hugged me. I pulled away from her and tears were rolling down her cheeks rapidly. She was panting uncontrollably and shaking like a leaf.

"Layla, what's wrong? What happened?" I asked, trying to calm her down.

"It's Jack!" She cried.

"What about him?"

"He's gone!

18

A FORGOTTEN REALM

~~~

"So, one moment he's dying in bed, and the next he's gone?" I questioned Layla as we sat in Jack's bedroom confused.

"I left him for two seconds to change his head cloth, and when I came back, he was gone!" Layla explained, worried.

"What a great thing to come back to..." I murmured.

I was sick and tired of people disappearing at this point, it was just getting old. Charissa, my father, Fertility, all the other gods and now Jack. Don't get me wrong, I was really worried, but it didn't make sense to me. He is from earth, magic-less and unfamiliar with Atlasdam. Where could have he run off to this time? We were all worried about Jack, but there was nothing we could do other than dropping everything and looking for him, which we didn't have time for. We all agreed that we put this aside for now and deal with one problem and time.
~~~

Layla wasn't completely happy with this but she soon understood.

We gathered in the war room and Therion rolled out a large map on the table.

"Your majesty, I found this in your mother's old study." He said and began placing books on each corner of the map to keep it down."

I sat up in my chair and examined the map. At the very top of the parchment read out 'Althea' in wavy writing. It was a map of my mother's realm. It was quite a large city and very symmetrical by the looks of it. The palace stood in the middle of the realm and both sides mirrored the other exactly.

"When was this map drawn up?" I asked.

"I can't say for sure your majesty, I apologize." He said, sounding disappointed.

"Don't worry about it." I told him. "Does anyone have any ideas how we can do this carefully?" I asked looking at everyone but no one looked very confident.

"Well considering we don't know what we're up against, no." Alfyn stated.

He was too right. We had no idea what we were dealing with and what was going on in Althea as we spoke. All we knew was that all the universe's gods dwelled there, but for what reason? Was there some disturbance in the cosmos that had to be dealt with all the gods at once? Maybe a godly council meeting, but why would such a thing last for months? It made me fear that we were dealing with something far worse, bigger than all of us. The passage from the book of prophecies popped into my head.

"A boy of Revenge and Love, will pierce the heart of Malice and vanquish the beckoning Darkness summoned by a mysterious foe."

I couldn't help but feel that it had some relevance to what has been happening. Me being the 'boy of Revenge and Love' made me wonder my place in all this. How are my mother and father wrapped up in all this? One is dead and one is missing, so how would either of them know?

"Did my father ever mention anything about me Therion? Did he ever talk to you about that prophecy?"

"Your father spoke of a lot of things, but he couldn't bear to talk about such a manner while you were still missing. But he did spend quite a bit of time studying ancient rituals and other sorts of old magic." Therion explained.

"Your dad and I tried practicing a few spells ourselves." Ophilia added. "Ones that could show us where Medusa had taken you before we had Hastings make the compass. He also looked into curing your mother if we found her."

"How exactly did you practice that?" I queried.

"Well, he said he gathered the ashes of the snake that bit your mother to analyse them, and when I was of age, he recruited me to help him since I was top of my class. We were able to extract the same evil that corrupted your mother. We tested them on some animals and all of them went completely nuts."

"And could you cure them?" I asked with hope.

She shook her head in disappointment. I felt the same but it didn't even matter if my mother could have been cured, she's dead, and she's not coming back. I constantly hated admitting it to myself but it was the only thing I could do from being distracted by the past. The more I mourned over what has happened, the more ignorant I would be of what is happening. I needed to be the leader my friends needed to be. The prince that will lead my realm out of the darkness and back into the light.

"We need a battle plan. We need to get into the city without attracting unwanted attention so we can reach the palace without too much trouble. Does my grandmother rule Althea?"

"I'm afraid we know no more than you, your

majesty." Therion pointed out. "Atlasdam and Althea were connected closely. But a few days after you disappeared, they cut off communication with us. We theorized that it was connected to your mother's corruption."

So many things weren't adding up. My mother gets corrupted. She already has a palace and forces in the underworld. Medusa speaks of a ritual and she needs them "all" for it to commence. All of what? She also mentions her 'master'. Who could it be? Who is really pulling the strings behind all of this? I had a sick feeling that we would find out in Althea.

"Well, whatever it is, we have to be prepared."

Everyone nodded their heads in agreement. We all gathered around the map and came up with a way to get into Althea undetected.

"We will open the portal here." I said and pointed to an area far from the city on the map.

"Ophilia and Serenity will fly in on a Pegasus to see what we are up against." They both nodded and listened carefully. "Look for things that could be a problem. Catapults, ballistae."

"What if the city has a magic barrier?" Serenity asked.

"I'm pretty sure my father had spells on force field penetration." I clarified.

"Once you come back with information, we go from there."

"Ray, we have no idea what we're flying into!" Layla disputed. "It's like walking into an exam room and not having studied the night before."

"How do you suggest we study for this?!" I argued. "We know absolutely nothing about Althea and what is happening there. Every God in the universe is there and we don't know why. That's why we have to be careful. We're dealing with gods. We could either be safe, or in huge danger if we go."

"He's right." Serenity commended. "There's nothing else we can do but be careful on this mission. My mother and Raven's father are there. Whether they are alright or not, we have to go."

"You know I'm always up for a bit of danger, but I don't know about this one. All the gods in one place..." Alfyn fretted. "I have seen what Triton is capable of, and if that is used against us, we don't stand a chance."

"Then you see why we have to go. If something has happened to the gods, every realm will suffer. And if that power is used for evil, the results could be catastrophic. "I explained. "I know you're all scared and confused, but it's what we need to do in order to protect everything Zeus created. He created these worlds, and he trusted his gods to protect them. And those gods aren't here right now, so it's up to us. It's up to us to bring an end to all this madness. So....are you with me or not?

They all looked at each other waiting for someone to respond.

"You know I'm in." Serenity beamed and smiled at me warmly. "For Leafstonia and my mother."

Therion stepped forward and gave me a supporting look. "For my king and prince."

"I'm with you till' the end Ray." Layla cheered and stood with us.

Ophilia and Alfyn stood before us with uneasy eyes. I saw their brains churning, processing the decision they were about to make. But inevitably they stepped forward also.

"For Raven."

"Thank you everyone. Now suit up! We have a realm to investigate!" I ordered.

We headed to the palace armory and geared ourselves up with the best armor possible. I wore a black Atlian battle robe with silver shoulder pads, arm guards and thick metal boots. Serenity tied up her long blonde hair and used her magic to create clothes from hardwood and thorny vines. She looked like her mother's statue in the center of Leafstonia, beautiful as always.

Ophilia chanted a long spell and when she finished a blue bubble surrounded and then molded itself around her, then disappearing but she glowed slightly.

"Protective armor." she said with much confidence and I smiled impressed.

Alfyn opened an official looking cupboard in the armory and revealed a set of armor made of a bright green metal.

"This is what my father wore in combat when he was my age. He always said I was free to use it. It is magically modified to fit around whatever animal we become when we transform." He explained as he gazed at the masterpiece.

"Speaking off..." I spoke. "Any luck on unlocking your magic?"

He shook his head but he wasn't disappointed. "I don't need magic. I mean I sure would like it but I don't need it. Not when I got this!" he said a pulled out a small golden stick from his pocket. He swung it to his side and it instantly converted into a blade. Its hilt was made of gold and the blade was a transparent green magic. It glowed on the floor as

Alfyn held it sureness.

"Where the hell did you get that?" I asked in confusion but also impressed.

"Hastings made it for me. It can turn into a bow and shield too. It's three weapons in one!" He squealed.

"When he saw someone in Coldera using it he practically begged Hastings to make it for him." Ophilia called out from the other side of the room and sniggered.

"Hey I need something to protect myself with, don't I? You guys all have magic and I'm here with nothing. But now that I have this thing I can be as good as any of you guys."

"Alf' you have always been amazing." I urged. "You're in the royal guard at the age of seventeen. You helped Therion watch over my home while me and father were absent from the throne. You put up with Hastings's crap because you were so determined to help me bring back my father. So don't think for one second that not having powers lowers the respect you deserve."

"Thanks man, really hit it here." Alfyn marveled and beat his chest with a clenched fist.

I patted him on the back but my eye caught a glimpse of Layla struggling in the corner. I walked over to her and she couldn't decide what to wear and arm herself with.

"Sorry I'm not really used to going to a magical war." She huffed and looked at me for an answer. She sat in front of a rack of weapons that all had different abilities. Some were good for close combat, some for long range.

"You know I felt exactly the same way sitting in Gym class back at school. I would hold a tennis racket thinking it was some kind of weapon to defend myself." I told her.

"Is that why you launched a tennis ball at Ryan?" She asked sarcastically.

"That's not what I'm trying to get at. What I'm saying is I had no idea how to properly prepare myself in a brand-new world. But you know what I did? I applied what I *was* good to what I thought would work."

"So, what you're saying is that I should think about what I'm good at in Gym class and apply it here?" She guessed.

"I mean kind of. What was that spinney stick thing you were twirling around?" I uncertainly asked.

"You mean a Baton?" She said and looked at me as if I was joking.

"Yeah, so why don't you just imagine twirling one of them while using this?" I said and handed her a short pole. "Press the button in the middle."

She stood up and pressed the button on the pole and a blade came out of each end of the pole.

"It's a double ended spear. Just imagine that it's your baton thing," I reassured.

She fiddled with it and held it tightly. She looked up at me and forced a smile.

"Thanks ray. I'm sorry for being all negative Nancy, it's just I'm really worried about Jack."

"Come on now." I said and sat down beside her. "Jack lost both of his parents, went through years of abuse from his alcoholic uncle and ran away from the only world he understood. He's one of the strongest people I have ever met. He will be fine."

"Yeah, but the last thing we did was fight, what if I never see him again? I have to live with that for the rest of my life. He's like a brother to me." Layla cried.

"I still don't understand what was up with him before, but I can guarantee that when we find him, he will come around."

Layla laid her head on my shoulder and rubbed her eyes. "Is there ever a time where you aren't this soft?" She joked.

I put my arm around her and rubbed her gently. "Well, I was in literal hell for ten years." I joked back.

"Yeah, and I lost my parents in a yacht sinking."

"Well then I guess we're both softies." I mocked. We both sat up and smiled. We were lucky to have each other.

I went out the palace gardens one more time before we left. It was the last place I wanted to see if I never came back from Althea. I let the nostalgia fill me up while I took deep breaths through the nose to smell every scent from every flower. I walked deeper into the gardens but I noticed I wasn't the only one enjoying the scenery. Serenity sat on her knees in the soft grass, making the flowers dance with her magic. I always knew she would be fascinated by all the wonders of this garden. After all, she was the daughter of the Goddess of nature. I watched her for a bit before I spoke to her. The flowers moved in sync with the movement she made with her fingers. Her connection between her and nature was amazing. Serenity dug her hands into the dirt and channeled her powers into the earth itself. Slowly, flowers bloomed from tiny saplings in the ground and grew into beautiful green petaled roses. They matched her eyes. She took her hands out from the ground and closed her left above the small batch of flowers she just bloomed. She opened her hand again and revealed a clump of sparkly pink dusk in her palm.

She brought her hand to her face and blew the dust all over the flowers. Now they sparkled in the sun. She was so creative. She got to her feet but she tripped after taking a step but I caught her with my magic. She looked around to see who casted it and saw me sitting on the fountain. I levitated her over and sat her down. She smirked at me.

"Like what you see?" I cooed.

"What you? Or the garden?" She jessed and grinned.

"I guess we both had the same idea in coming here." I conversed.

"Yes, this place is amazing. It reminds me of home. And the statue of you and your mother...I'm so sorry you had to endure all that Raven." She said and turned to me. "But if we bring your father back; it might fill that hole in your heart."

The feeling that I felt when Serenity looked into my eyes and related to me on a different level was all I needed to fill that hole. Her presence was comforting and I never wanted it to end. Her kindness was sweet but I loved her casual sarcasm. I think I knew what I felt but I didn't know how to put it into words. But they say actions speak louder than words...

We were so close and I wanted to feel her embrace. My hands met her warm cheek and I closed my eyes.

"Ehm sorry to interrupt..." Therion interrupted.

I thought it was impossible to be mad at Therion, but I was proven wrong.

"Yes, Therion?" I pulled away from Serenity and we were both flustered.

"Well firstly your highness, you're making everything float in the air..." He began.

I looked around me and Therion was right. Pots, shovels, even the very water from the fountain was floating, surrounded by my red aura. I cut off all my power and everything fell back down, us being splashed by the water. I guess Serenity was right when she said our emotions impact our magic.

"Secondly," Therion continued. "We're about to set off to Althea, everyone is boarding the A.S Destiny." He finished and walked away.

Me and Serenity both looked at each other with red cheeks and giggled at the embarrassment. We walked to the A.S Destiny together, holding hands. We gazed at each other frequently as we made our way to the ship. The butterflies in me only fluttered more with each gaze. I was upset that Therion ruined our moment, but I was delighted that I got closer to Serenity. I was happy that we will be able to finish this together. It only felt like yesterday when we met and I first set my red eyes into her shiny emeralds. She looks at me like no one else does and I treasured every smile that appeared on her stunning face. I got so distracted while we smiled at each other that I didn't even notice Alfyn talking to me.

"Raven. Raven!" he yelled.

I broke from Serenity's smile and acted like nothing happened. "Yeah, what's going on?"

"Are you coming?"

"Yes, sorry. There was a....bug on Serenity's face." I choked. I felt my face go bright red and Serenity giggled at me. "Let's set off."

Serenity made branches grow beneath our feet and they lifted us to the ships deck. Therion looked at me and grinned. That's when I remembered he could read minds, making me even more flustered. I walked by him and his grin remained, but he already knew what I was thinking, so he said nothing.

I stationed myself at the ship's helm and grasped the wheel firmly. I pulled the level and the ship slowly levitated into the sky. We waited until we ascended to an appropriate altitude and I looked over my home one more time. I promised to try all I could to return to it, but I knew it was a promise I wouldn't be able to guarantee. I would bring my father back no matter what the cost, and restore normality to this mad universe Zeus created. I looked over to Therion and I gave him the signal. He waved his hand at the empty sky and the sparkle of a portal formed before us.

I pushed the lever forward and the ship propelled forward. My eyes laid upon my kingdom one last time before we entered, hoping to see the sun set on it again. We crossed through and finally entered the realm of Althea, and it was not all what I expected. I pictured a realm filled with life and prosperity, but all we saw was darkness and lifelessness. No green grass, no blue sky. It was like all life had been drained, just like the bush my father described. The same bush that the snake that bit my mother jumped out of. Grey, dark, lifeless. The sun was silver and casted a bleeding shadow onto the already dark realm. This confirmed my conjecture, this wasn't a 'cosmic meeting'.

We caught a glimpse of the kingdom as we flew and it seemed to be the only place in the entire realm that had life in it. It was colorful but quiet, which was odd for a big city. Also, Serenity was right about the barrier. The city was protected by a powerful looking transparent purple force field.

Luckily Ophilia had a spell just for that. But first we needed to go do a bit of reconnaissance. We found a big enough hill to hide the Destiny behind and landed without drawing attention.

"Well, this sure is splendid." Alfyn denounced. "They should have a greeting card for Althea. 'Come for the holiday of a lifetime, nowhere else like it in the universe.' He bantered.

"Alfyn I'm sure there's a reason behind all this." Therion assured. "Your father never talked about the queen's realm, Raven. But I'm almost certain it wouldn't look like this." He began examining a dark grey tree with black leaves and looked almost horrified.

"I can't feel a thing." Serenity whimpered. "I can usually feel the life around me but..." The fear on her face grew and she fell to her knees. My instincts reacted and I dashed over to her and held her in my arms. "It's a terrible feeling...Like everything you once knew has been zapped like water to a flame."

"Yeah, I know the feeling." I said and pulled her up. "But you have to overcome it for now. It must feel awful to not feel that vibration around you, but we have to keep going. We're so close and we can't allow such a thing to get the better of us. You're strong, you'll be okay." I said and winked.

"Well let's go then." Ophilia called out from the

ship. She pressed a button at the helm and a door I had no idea about opened at the back of the ship to reveal Ophilia and Serenity's ride, a white stallion Pegasus. She was a majestic creature with long feathery wings and a shiny silver mane. Serenity approached her and gently stroked her face and she neighed slightly.

“Mount up Ophilia.”

19

A CITY OF FORGOTTEN SOULS

~~~

The girls took to the skies with Serenity in the front. The rest of us had the boring job of waiting for them to return with info. Layla wanted to try and watch them so she climbed to the top of the hill and crouched down so she wouldn't be seen. Therion was curious about all the plant life being dead so he began taking samples and examined them on the ship. Jack and I decided to train together for a bit because we thought it would be good to know each other's skills. But really because Alfyn desperately wanted to try out the new toy Hastings made for him.

"Don't hold back." He boasted and went into a fighting stance

I channeled my magic into a ball of energy and launched it at him. In a quick succession he swung his stick and it transformed into a shield, and blocked my blast.

"Impressive, but are you ready for...this?!" I
~~~

levitated a rock and hurled it at Alfyn. He swung his shield and it folded into his sword. He struck the rock with the blade and split it in two.

"This thing is amazing." Alfyn squealed. "Try harder!"

I channeled more power around me and blasted him a few more times but he deflected each blast. I lifted three rocks and hurled them at him. He swung his shield and it folded into a bow. He flipped backwards dodging the first one and whilst midair, he drew two arrows on his bow and shot the last two rocks with explosives. He landed perfectly on his feet and left us all shell shocked.

"Just like his father." Therion said.

"Guys, they're coming back!" Layla called out from the hill.

Our eyes shot to the sky as we saw the winged stallion coming in for a landing. A gust of wind rustled my hair as the Pegasus flapped its wings. Serenity and Ophilia climbed off and they had worried looks.

"This isn't going to be easy."

We assembled around the desk in the captain's quarters of the Destiny. Therion rolled out the map of Althea so Serenity and Ophilia could show us what we were up against.

"The barrier around the city is strong." Ophilia began. "It's possible to break through but it will be tough. I'll need someone else's power to help me channel enough energy to break it."

"I can assist you there Ophilia." Therion added.

"Also, when we break through, we have to be quick. It will probably close up the second we make an opening so we have to fly through as fast as possible."

"What about defenses?" Alfyn asked. "Have they got canons or anything that might cause trouble?"

"Well, they do have ballistae. Ten or fifteen of them. All mounted on the wall wrapped round the city." Serenity said.

"Well then Alfyn can take out the gunner and-"

"No that's the thing...none of them have gunners. They control themselves," Serenity pointed out.

We all looked at each other confused. Something like that isn't impossible, but where was all this magic coming from. Althea couldn't be that advanced to generate a full barrier around the city and self-shooting ballistae. Where was all this power coming from? But then I remembered why we were here. Maybe it was the gods, maybe they didn't want us to enter the city and this is how they're stopping us. Well, I knew a few ballistae and a barrier wasn't going to stop me from seeing my father.

"We dodge the fire from each ballista while Therion and Ophilia channel the power to break the barrier. Then when they break it open, we fly through safely." I explained.

"I can draw the fire from the ballistae on the Pegasus as well as you." Alfyn offered.

"Sounds good. Just be careful." I added.

"I always am." He joshed.

"Right then, let's do this."

We all boarded the Destiny and flew directly towards the city, prepared to risk our lives for our gods. Alfyn flew on the Pegasus beside us but split from us as we got close. We got within range of the ballistae and they reacted to our presence. Serenity and Ophilia were right, they were completely automated. I flew the ship closer and a ballista shot a bright purple arrow made of a thick looking aura.

"You better grab hold of something!" I called out to everyone and they all held on to the nearest thing.

My hands gripped the wheel of the helm and spun it, the ship hurling to the left, dodging the arrow. Chips claws dug into my shoulder as he held onto me tightly. I plucked him from my shoulder and carefully placed him into the front pocket of my robe, his head sticking out slightly. As the ship glided through they looked down and saw Alfyn attracting the fire, giving Ophilia and Therion the time they needed.

Therion looked at me and I knew he read my mind because he reacted as soon as I thought of it. Serenity tied them to the ship with vines so they wouldn't be knocked around as we flew. The two held hands and began chanting the spell. A blue glowing aura formed and whirled around them. Another Ballista shot at us but I spun the wheel, dodging it.

"How long will this take?!" I yelled as I tried hard to concentrate on steering the ship.

Therion and Ophilia were still reciting the spell so Serenity responded for them. "Ophilia said it could take up to two minutes until enough energy- look out!" she warned.

An arrow shot right before nearly grazing my face. All the ballistae were aiming at me and Alfyn. Many magic arrows were fired and I flew the best I could, but one arrow skimmed the side of the Destiny and wood parts came flying off.

"Raven, can you try and maybe steer us *away* from the deadly magic arrows!?" Layla screamed through the sound of the loud wind.

"Do you think I want us to get shot out of the sky?!" I yelled back. "We need to be close so we get through the barrier in time."

Things started heating up. The firing pattern became more unpredictable and rapid. Alfyn was doing his best to draw the fire, but they were mainly focused on the large flying ship rather than a tiny Pegasus. One arrow shot in my direction but I deflected it with a magic shield, but the speed of the arrow knocked me back and I lost hold of the helm, no one was steering the ship. Another arrow shot at us and hit the mast, completely causing it to completely shatter. I struggled to get to my feet and take control of the ship but Layla jumped into action and grabbed it herself. She turned the wheel and dodged an arrow that would have hit us.

"This is easier than it looks!" She boasted.

"Make sure to stay close to the barrier. I'm going to try and provide some protection while Ophilia and Therion finish the spell." I called out and ran down to the middle of the ship.

I stood directly where the mast was and held my hands out wide. I channeled my power around me and imagined what I wanted vividly in my mind. The magic surged through my entire body and I lashed it out beyond me. A red transparent aura began surrounding the A.S Destiny, protecting it from the arrows. But with every strike from the large magic arrows, I felt like I was being struck directly.

"Guys if you can hear me, please hurry it up! I don't know how long I can hold this!" I called out through the pain I was feeling from channeling this much magic

The blue magic was swirling around them even more. But suddenly everything stopped and they finished chanting. They opened their eyes and they shone bright blue.

"Layla! bring us in closer!" Therion called out.

Layla brought the ship towards the barrier and Alfyn knew it was time so he flew up to us and landed the Pegasus on the deck. Therion held out his left hand and Ophilia held out her right, both pointing at the barrier. As they had their hands held out, they said gently 'Brackaro'. Suddenly an insane bright blast of energy erupted from their hands and fired at Althea's barrier. Ophilia and Therion collapsed but Serenity's vines caught them. There was an unfathomably loud smashing sound, as if a million glass bottles smashed at once when the blast connected with the barrier. A large hole formed in the purple shield, but it was already starting to close...

"Layla step on it!" I shouted and I let down my shield, extremely weak from it.

Layla pushed the accelerator as far it could go and the ship sped towards the city at full speed. The barrier was getting smaller and smaller. It didn't look like we're going to make it, but the bow of the ship reached the other side, but that was short-lived. An arrow shot right into the Destiny and penetrated it right through. The aircraft was about to make a very unpleasant landing. The entire ship made it through the barrier, but it began falling from the sky.

We all panicked as the ship hurled through the sky with us trying to hold the best we could. The memories of when I escaped the Underworld and appeared on earth flashed in my mind. When I was falling from the sky on a broken airship, my life flashing before me. The wind in my face, the tears trickling down, it was all the same in this moment, but I was happy to have my friends there with me in my final moments. I couldn't stop the ship because I used all my strength protecting it. There was nothing I could do. The ground was getting very close very fast. But suddenly I felt tightness around me. Vines began wrapping around my entire body and then I noticed the same was happening to everyone else. They were protecting us. It was Serenity. I held onto chip in my front pocket before my arms were wrapped. The vines wrapped themselves around my head and I could barely see through the small gap in them. The ship was close to hitting the ground. I held tightly onto chip and closed my eyes, preparing for the impact. The ship collided with the ground and I was knocked unconscious.

Complete darkness, a familiar scene, and I hear the woman's voice again. The same voice that told me.

"Find me Raven. Find me and we can do this together...".

The voice was faint but it started to become clear. "You're almost here. Come and we can do this together." Tt said in a sterner manner but playfully at the same time.

"Raven!" came another voice, but I knew this voice.

I gained consciousness and saw Layla before me. She looked worried but relieved when I opened my eyes.

"Oh, thank god, he's alright!" Therion announced.

Layla sat me up and my eyes began to focus.

My head was pounding with pain. "What happened?" I asked as I held my head in my hand.

"Don't worry about that for now, just rest." Serenity said.

With my eyes fully focused at this point, I noticed Serenity's arm was in a sling made of branches and leaves. She had blood dripping from her forehead and eyebrow. I noticed that she wasn't the only one injured. Alfyn's hand was in a cast made of sticks and Therion's head was wrapped in vines.

"I'm guess we had a nasty crash." I said and felt my front pocket for chip, but he wasn't there. "Where's Chip!" I panicked.

"Don't worry, he's here." Ophilia called out and I saw him sitting in her cupped hands. He looked around at me with his dark eyes with curiosity and I was relieved to see him safe.

"What happened to the Destiny?" I asked.

Layla looked at me sadly.

"You're sitting in it." Alfyn choked.

I looked around and saw many broken planks of wood scattered around us. The helm was without the wheel, and at my foot was on top of the gold plate that read 'The A.S Destiny'. It was all gone. The ship that took us so far. The vessel that carried us across the universe, back to my home. It was gone just like that. The sadness in me grew and consumed my eyes with tears. I felt like I had lost a part of me. The beacon of hope that would fly us to end, and it did just that, it served its purpose in destiny itself.

"I'm so sorry Raven. At least she served you well." Therion comforted.

"You know I never understood why people call their ships 'she'." Ophilia wondered.

"Most people name their ships after the most important people in our lives." Alfyn explained. "Mothers, wives, daughters. It's the people we cherish the most. So, people name their ships so they are always with them."

"Yeah, that's great and everything but are we just going to ignore the fact that we are in the same city as every god in the universe?" Serenity gripped.

"Sorry I was just trying to lighten the mood."

"I don't mean to be blunt. It's just we have come this far and we can't stop to vent about ships."

Serenity's words hurt a bit, but I understood her frustration. I was absolutely devastated about the Destiny, but I would be even more devastated if we didn't keep going after all this time."

"Where are we anyway?" I asked and looked around.

From the looks of it, it seemed we crashed into a house. Not only was there wood from the ship, but there was stone and glass. I saw a broken picture frame and a shredded couch. I looked up and saw the small remnants of a brick roof, and the purple barrier above that. Layla helped me get to my feet but a shock of pain spiked through my leg and I fell into her arms. I looked down and my leg was between two splints tied together with vines.

"You broke your leg when we crashed." Serenity said. "I tried to patch you up the best I could but there wasn't much I could do."

"It's okay, I can manage. You did a great job helping everyone." I commended and gave a supporting smile.

We all exited the ship's wreckage, but before we paid our respects, Serenity planted a small memorial filled with flowers, and in the middle, we put the gold name plate.

My leg was killing me but I wasn't going to let that stop me. We ventured the empty streets of Althea, not one person to be seen. But every now and then we would catch a glimpse of someone dashing down an alleyway or closing their curtains when they saw us limp down the street. The people lived in fear, but of what? I tried asking a man in the street but he was scared out of his mind and ran. He was covered in a raggedy cloak and carrying a small wooden crate. When I saw his face, it was white and I could see his cheek bones bulging out of his skin. He looked weak and starved. When he ran, he dropped the box and a small amount of food rolled off it, bread, and vegetables. But the food didn't look healthy at all. The break was almost green and had mold growing out of it and the vegetables were shriveled and rotted to the core. I called out to him to give it back to him but he was too far gone.

We limped further and we could see the tip of the palace behind the buildings. We began going in that direction but as we got closer, I could feel a strong vibration inside of me, as if it was pulling me. I felt this feeling before when I found the prophecy in the library. It was like I was getting closer to the answer to everything, like it was falling into place.

After we dragged ourselves through the city and made it to the palace entrance, the feeling was stronger than ever now. The palace was made of a purple stone, the same purple that surrounded the city. It was tall and loomed over everything. But as we approached it, we realized that there was the same scarcity of guards as there were citizens. not a single guard to stop us. This was odd because you would think the gods or whoever is really behind this would have some decent security. Then again, maybe they thought no one could get through that force field. But us being the heroines we are, got through it with only minimal struggle. Losing a ship and a few bones along the way.

We trekked up the tall stone staircase that led up to the malicious structure, each step making everything more intense. But I had a misstep and tripped on the stairs, sending extreme pain through my broken leg. Serenity held my arm and sat me down gently on a step.

“I'm fine, let's just keep going.” I said, trying to ignore the pain.

“Raven stop and rest for a moment.” Serenity demanded.

“I said I'm fine. Let's keep going.” I stubbornly argued. “We're almost there, the entrance is literally right-.”

“We’ve walked for miles and that’s not good on your leg.” Layla stepped in.

“Listen I understand that you're afraid of what lies ahead,” Therion said, ``I knew he had just read my mind. “And I understand that you want to stare your fear dead in the face, but you need to stop for one moment and realize that what you're about to walk into could potentially risk everything we have worked so hard to protect.”

“Listen to him Ray, you know he’s right.” Alfyn added.

“He probably does as well.” I said under my breath and looked at Therion. I knew he was inventively reading me like a book, but I knew his intentions were pure. I saw it in his eyes as the psychedelic magic twinkled inside of them.

Suddenly I heard Therion's voice, but his lips remained shut. He was making me hear him.

"I feel it too." His voice echoed in my mind.

"The pull?" I thought.

"Yes. It's strong, and it's calling us, although I don't yet know what it means."

"Then that's why we have to keep going! We need to put a stop to all of this. Look at the people in this realm. Their suffering because of all of this."

"Raven, your father entrusted me with the responsibility of finding you and protecting you. I can feel the conflict in you and I understand wanting to fix everything you have lost." I heard.

"How could you possibly understand that? How could you understand losing everything you ever had in one day?" I angrily thought.

"Because I have lost everything once before..." his voice said.

My mind went blank and the confusion sat as I waited for him to continue. could Therion be telling the truth, or could he just be saying this to distract me?

"I was your age, and I was still learning to control

my unique and powerful gift. I was happy with my family in the realm of Stonekeep. But just like you, on one faithful day, I lost everything in a matter of seconds. It was late one night, and I was returning home from a stressful day of magic practice and I was on edge because of the day I had. All I desired was to go home and relax, but that wasn't what I came home to. My mother and father were fighting. My younger siblings were causing trouble and the house was chaotic. I tried to sit down and ignore it all, but it was all cutting into me deep. The shouting, the screaming, the crying, it was all too much for me to handle, and as you know, our emotions greatly affect our magic.

"The stress was making me sweat; the sweat was making me itch; my blood was boiling; my eyes were twitching and my mind was flooded with everyone else's chaotic thoughts. Eventually I broke, and so did my magic. My magic lashed onto everyone else around me. My mother, my father, and my younger siblings, began feeling excruciating pain because I couldn't control my power. It couldn't be stopped; my emotions were too out of control. I felt their pain and heard their thoughts as they shrieked in my mind. All I could do was watch as they suffered, and soon after…. killed. I killed them…." Therion's voice echoed in my head, the guilt setting in his eyes as he looked at me.

The thought of something so gruesome happening

to a person like Therion never once crossed my mind. He was always well put out and regal, but no one ever knew that he had such a dark past. He lost everything in a matter of seconds, everyone he loved…gone forever. That must have been the reason he never told anyone about it because he was afraid of hurting anyone else with his magic. I'm not the only person that has suffered in this universe, and I know that more than ever now. I have taken what I love for granted and I was so blind to the risks that I was putting my friends in harm to fix what I have lost…

I broke away from Therion's gaze and sat up. "I'm sorry everyone. I have taken you all for granted. You have been there for me at my lowest, and I never once showed my appreciation. And now we're here, all in danger, all because of my obsession to fix the past."

Layla sat down beside me and put her arm on my shoulder. "Raven Griffin, you're loyal, caring and overall, an extraordinary person. You have shown me things that I could never even dream of. But don't let your arrogance cloud the greatness in you. I'm sure Jack would say the same."

That's when the guilt hit me the most, I had completely forgotten about Jack. What has happened to him?

"I'm sure Jack is fine wherever he is." Therion said.

He knew what I was thinking.

"But what if something bad has happened to him?" I responded in fear.

"I think we're going to find out soon enough." Ophilia chimed in. "Look." She pointed at the palace entrance and we all turned around to see a familiar face.

"Jack!" Layla cried out.

There he was standing at the stop of the stairs, but he was different. I couldn't see him very well but it wasn't the Jack I knew before. His aura was more down than usual and the spark in his confident eyes had gone out. He was dressed in a dark black armor and held a frightening blade in his hand.

"Jack where have you been?!" Layla called out. But he said nothing and walked away, into the palace as if he owned it.

"What is he doing?" Layla said and went to go after him but Alfyn stopped her.

"Hold up, we don't know what's wrong with him. Let's all go together, that's if you're up to it Ray." He asked and held out his hand.

I grabbed it firmly and he pulled me to my feet.

The end was upon us, and I felt it now more than ever.

20

A LABYRINTH OF DECEIT

~~~

We dragged our injured bodies up the stone stairs and reached the large doors to the palace of Althea. The pull reached right at my very core and it was calling me even further. I had my friends beside me and I was ready to face whatever the universe threw at me. Ophilia did the honors of opening the doors as she waved her staff at the door and her blue power covered it. She thrusted her arm forward and the doors opened with it. I winked at her and she smirked. We looked down the long eerie hallway that led into the palace. We all linked hands and braced ourselves for anything that could happen. I took a deep breath and stepped inside. The pulling on my heart stopped completely and I felt nothing but the agonizing pain in my leg. I turned around to see the outside one more time in fear of never seeing it again, however, the doors were gone, like they were never there.

"Is it just me or did there used to be a door here?"
~~~

Everyone else turned around and realized the missing entrance we had just come through. Serenity held my arm tighter. I looked at her and she looked scared as she processed the fact that we were trapped. I placed my index finger under her chin and moved her gaze towards mine.

"We're going to be okay." I comforted.

An uneasy smile appeared on her face and that filled with a small amount of confidence. Chip peaked out from my pocket and to see where we were, and he looked just as scared and returned to the safety of my pocket.

The palace was dimly lit by torches doused with a purple flame, creating an uneasy atmosphere. Along the walls there were vein line vessels of magic, and they looked like they were pulsing, in a painfully creepy way. Then Therion stopped and the magic in his silver eyes began swirling.

"What's going on Therion?" Ophilia asked.

He hesitated before speaking, as if he was struggling. "This place…I can feel it. It's it's…. alive."

"What do you mean it's alive?" Alfyn queried.

"I can hear whispering in my mind, it's calling for

Raven..." He said and looked at me.

"Why would it be calling for me?" My spine quivered as these words escaped my mouth.

"I don't know, but they really want you to '*find them*'." He processed.

"Is it a female voice?" I asked.

"Yes." He answered.

"Then it must be the same voice I heard in the library on earth and in my dream. She's here..."

"It's all coming together..." Serenity she shivered.

Whoever this shadowy enigma was, they have caused enough damage and fear to too many people. I wasn't going to let them be a threat to this world or any other anymore. Whoever they are, wherever they are....it ends now...

We kept going and the further we got, the louder the pulsing became. Therion was getting agitated because of the constant whispers in his head and he said they also became louder the further we went. He asked us to stop after a while and said that the whispers were extremely loud and he left like we were getting close. At first, we didn't believe him. The reason being is we turned a corner and we were met by the same set of doors we entered the palace through, the same set that disappeared about an hour ago.

"So we're back where we started. Brilliant." Layla smirked.

"No, we are where we're meant to be, the whisper says so." Therion told us.

"But we already came through these doors, they will just lead outside." Alfyn added.

"I wouldn't say that." Ophilia said. "This place is filled with illusion magic and they're more likely to lead us somewhere else."

"She's right, I can feel it." Therion said looking more agitated than ever. "This person is close.

There was only one thing left to do then...We open the doors and face whatever is on the other side. Ophilia and I both channeled our magic onto the door and flung it open. When we revealed what was on the other side, we weren't shocked by what was there, we were shocked at what wasn't there. It was complete blackness in an empty abyss of nothingness. We stepped into it and the door closed behind us again, followed by it disappearing. This place wasn't dark as we could all still see each other. The walls, the floors and ceiling were all pitch black. It sent shivers down my spine and the hairs on the back of my neck stood thin as I prepared myself for anything.

"The whispering stopped...We're here." Therion said and it boomed through the abyss

"Where is here exactly?" I said, trying to look beyond the darkness.

"Oh, so you finally made it!" An echoey voice came from nowhere, we all heard it.

Me and Therion shared a look and we both recognized it. It was her, the voice we have been hearing. Suddenly my non broken leg felt weak, but I felt brave as well as scared.

"Who are you and what have you done with my father!?" I shouted and it echoed in the nothing before me.

"And my mother!" Serenity shouted as well.

"Oh, don't worry about them, they're in good hands..." The voice said playfully. "You can see for yourself."

Suddenly the blackness began to fade and we started seeing the room we stood in, then I wish I hadn't when I saw what was in it. The room had come completely visible and I felt like I had been stabbed through the heart with shock, Serenity holding me up as I fell to my knees. Every single god seated around a long table. All with their eyes corrupted and drowned by the same blackness that once filled the room. I saw my father sitting near the top of the table and I shook violently. But who he was sitting beside was even more horrifying. He was sitting beside the devil that destroyed my life. Medusa. She was alive and well as if that cave never collapsed on her. I never thought I would find myself standing in her presence again. All of this was hitting me like several trains. My friends held me up as my legs failed to cooperate.

"Do you like your surprise Raven? It took you so long to finally listen to me and come here." The voice said and sent even more shivering throughout my body.

"Show yourself! Who are you!" I shrieked.

"Oh, you're still confused. Have a seat and we can have a little discussion, the rest of you can leave." She demanded.

"We're going nowhere!" Layla yelled.

I felt touched to have such amazing friends, but suddenly I fell to the ground, not feeling Serenity's hold anymore. I looked behind me and everyone had vanished, gone.

"Now that's it's just us, have a seat."

A sharp pain spiked down my leg when I tried to get up.

"Oh, you poor thing, let me help you."

My body levitated off the ground without my effort. I floated towards the table and was forcefully seated at the end surrounded by the black-eyed gods. I didn't recognize many of them but I felt unsettlingly uncomfortable. Every single one of them had dark grey skin, just like the plant life outside the barrier, like their life had been drained from them. They were all looking stone faced and lifeless. I wanted to get up and leave but I felt a presence appear behind me. I looked behind the chair and I sank into it deeper when I saw who it was. It was Jack, and he looked evenly more lifeless as the rest of the gods. His eyes were pitched with corruption and he looked at me as if had never seen me before.

"Jack! What's wrong with you?" I cried at him.

"I wouldn't bother with him. Even when he wasn't under my control he wouldn't have responded." the voice chuckled spitefully.

"I demand an explanation."

I said sternly and turned back in my chair. I peered down the table and saw a grand official looking chair that stood in the only bit of darkness left in the room. Then the darkness began to fade, revealing to me the person behind everything.

"What's wrong? You look like you have never seen your auntie, Pandora." she giggled.

I sat in shock and absolute confusion. This immoral, unholy devil was my aunt? She looked like something from a nightmare. Her eyes were dark purple but were filled with the same evil that flowed through the palace. Her veins were pulsing out of her skin, throbbing with power. She had long menacing black wings that arched out either side of her chair. She wore a dark magenta cloak that had the insides of a cosmic realm when you gazed into it. On her head she wore a devilish black crown bejeweled with glowing amethysts. Under it she had long brown locks that waved magically. In one hand, a bunch of chess pieces floated above her. In the other, she had glowing strings wrapped to all five fingers, like she was controlling a puppet. She looked extremely powerful as a purple aura swirled around her. She really had a thing for purple.

"How are you, my aunt?"

"I'm your mothers' sister of course! Isn't that right sis'?" She said and moved her fingers with the strings. Medusa nodded in rhythm with Pandora's finger movement. She was a puppet master, and these were her puppets. They were all under her control like mindless hollow shells.

"Why and how could you do something like this? What have these gods done to you?" I shuddered, reluctantly fearing the answer to this mania.

"Your mind is still young. My sister did abduct you when you were merely a child. Her evil heart was too important to leave dead, so I bought her back to help me. I have been disgraced my entire life, and it was all because of our mother. When I was eight, she sensed a dark presence inside me, so she called for Fortuna, goddess of Fortune. Fortuna read my future and showed my mother what '*could*' happen. I was fortunate to be the Goddess of Calamity. She saw chaos and devastation in my future. Apparently, I was part of some prophecy, the same prophecy you saw in that annoying little library."

The text of the prophecy popped into my head.

"A boy of Revenge and Love, will pierce the heart of Malice and vanquish the beckoning Darkness summoned by a mysterious foe."

"You're the mysterious foe summoning a darkness." I prophesied.

"Indeed. The next action my mother took only fulfilled it further. She was frightened by the fortune and wanted to put an end to it before it ever started. So, she imprisoned me. My own mother forgot about the eight years of love and cherishment, and banished me to the far corners of the universe. For almost two million years I was trapped and alone, all because my mother couldn't see the good me. Of course, I had time to think about my plan to get my revenge on the universe because my mother wasn't the only one to wave me out the door. Billions of people across the realms were relieved that the harbinger of chaos had been shunned for the greater good. But as you can see, that didn't really work out, did it?"

"You escaped and decided to wreak havoc." I guessed sarcastically.

"Well, aren't you a clever boy? The prison of insanity my mother trapped me in was powered by her own magic, and over the years her strength began to fade, giving me the opportunity I needed. The prison didn't stop me from using my power, it only contained it, meaning I had lots of time to practice my magic. One day I could sense my mother at her weakest, so that's when I tore down the barrier. I was free for the first time in 2 million years. And you thought you had it hard." She smirked.

"A snake corrupted my mother and tore my life apart!" I yelled and slammed my hands on the table.

"My own mother couldn't see the good in me, so she casted me out herself, not even caring what it would do to me. Believe me, you were meant to stay in the Underworld for more than ten years."

"What. What do you mean?" I gasped.

"Oh yeah, the snake biting your mother and her already having power in the Underworld...that was all courtesy of yours truly." She chortled and then sent a shrieking laugh throughout the palace.

Pandora was behind it all. Pandora caused my misery, all of it. We were simply pieces on a chess board for her to control.

"But wait, that's not even the best part!" She cackled. "When I escaped, I returned here to Althea and went after my mother. I stole her magic, leaving her powerless and decided to banish HER to a place she could never torment me ever again. I heard Rhea had gone and got herself married to the God of Revenge and ruled over one of the biggest realms in the universe. I knew she could have been useful so I sent that snake on her and turned the tides on the Goddess of Love. But there is always disappointment, she couldn't even keep a spineless mistake like you to stay put. I could have tracked you down the second you escaped, but the strange thing was that I couldn't. Something was stopping me from using my magic to find you."

"What sort of thing?"

I never figured out what it was. What could be strong enough to shield you from the combined power of the gods. I bugged the life out of me, but that you were only a minor setback. While you were rotting away in the Demonite mines, I was gathering my friends here and taking their power, using it for myself. You'd be surprised by the number of things you can do with the combined power of the gods at your disposal."

"Try me." I dared.

"Ooo feisty, I love it! Well after a while I could finally track you down, whatever was protecting you must have given up. But I still couldn't affect you directly for some reason. So, I tried to work around it. I was the one that sent that Leviathan after you, if it wasn't for me, it would have just stayed asleep. Remember when you destroyed the wheel in the Gateway Temple? Yeah, that wasn't you, that was me. Then I saw that magicless fool, Hastings, helping you pinpoint our location. I did have the plan to control him into making a device to destroy you. However, the second you arrived in Coldera, I no longer could. But I was able to overpower that feeble machine of his causing it to explode. Unfortunately, not before you were able to find out where I was. And while you were away, I thought it would be fun to corrupt those human friends of yours. The girl's heart was too pure, too full of life. Jack here was the perfect fit, filled with envy and spite.

I couldn't believe what I was hearing. Pandora was the game master controlling destiny like a chess match. The magic she possessed was far too powerful for anyone to go up against. The ridiculous defenses outside were all her doing and who knows what else she could do. But why has she been calling me?

"Where do I fit in all this?" I hesitantly asked.

"Let me show you." She said and grinned evilly.

Pandora closed her hand that had the floating chess pieces in it and they disappeared in her closed hand. With her hand closed she waved it over the table in front of her and slowly opened her hand. A sparkly grey mist dispersed over the table and revealed a marble black and white chessboard. There were pieces dotted around the board, but they weren't like ordinary chess pieces. I looked closely at the black pieces and every single one of them were on the far side of the board, each of them having their own attributes. I then realized that they were representing each god seated at the table. One had many snakes emerging from one of the piece's heads, that had to be Medusa. There was another with a beard, black wings, and horns, it was my father. In the middle of the board all alone was a single white piece. I knew it had to be me.

"You see Raven, whoever I have under my control, their piece appears on my board here, and I control them like the pawns they are." She snarked.

I sat in shock as these tiny chess piece gods stood around a tiny version of Pandora, looking just as menacing as herself. But as I looked at them, I noticed not all of the black pieces were representing the gods. One was wearing a white coat and holding a tiny staff. Another had its hair tied and holding a tiny bow. Then when I saw a blonde one covered in vines, I knew who they were. They were my friends! Ophilia, Alfyn, Layla, Jack, Therion and Serenity. They were on the black side!

"What have you done to my friends!" I shouted in anger. If they were on the black side, they must be under her control.

"Don't worry about them, they're fine." She didn't even care.

"If you-" I snapped and tried to get up but I soon found Jack's sword at my throat. I looked up and he didn't even make eye contact with those black pearls.

"Careful now, you don't want what you did to your mother to happen to you now, do you?" She threatened, Jack moving as she twined her fingers. My eyes glanced at the board in front of Pandora and I saw that the black piece representing Jack had moved to my lone white piece.

"What do you want with me then?" Trying to be wary of the sword below my neck.

"After you escaped my sister's clutches, I wanted to snuff out that fiery spirit before you put any more kinks in my plan. But then I realized that you could be useful. Not only does my sister's magic live in you, but that former power of revenge from your father has been passed on to you. That power is one the strongest universe, and it lives in your veins. You're the son of two gods. How else do you think you were able to power an entire ship to travel across the realms without it ever stopping?"

The words she spoke were ones I have asked myself before. I always did wonder how much power laid dormant inside me. My father did say I was destined to wield great power, but I haven't really seen that yet, and I was scared to realize that one day I could. If I could power a ship to travel millions of miles across the universe, who knows what I'm capable of.

"I sense fear in you." Pandora's voice echoed. "Join me. Join me and I'll help you control it. I'll release your father and you two can be happy once again."

I looked over at Triton, but he didn't look back. A single tear rolled down his face from the black jewel, over a scar and into his beard. I knew he was still in there, but that man on the inside, was not what was on the outside. As much as I wanted to be with my father again, I knew Pandora wouldn't fulfill what she promised. She would only use me for my power and then drop me like a broken toy

"No." I breathed.

"Have it your way." She condescended and twirled her intertwined fingers while looking into my soul. I looked at the chessboard and noticed my piece moving to the far side of the board. The room began to fade and I found myself in darkness.

21

A VOID OF LIES

~~~

Sitting in the darkness that surrounded me, I waited for something to happen. With little strength I had left, I tried to conjure a ball of light, but even that came apart of the void. I called out for my friends but my shriveled voice only echoed into the abyss. My leg stopped me from standing so I couldn't get up and walk away, not that I particularly wanted to. The idea to use my magic to float instead of walking came to mind, but that was easier said than done. My hands felt around for a solid surface other than the floor that I could lean against. Eventually I was able to pull myself and balance on one leg against a vertical surface.

I was still weak from the ship's crash but was able to muster enough strength to channel the magic I needed to float a foot in the air. Then all I had to do was find a way out of this labyrinth. Wandering through the darkness isn't the same as wandering through darkness with your friends at your side. The fear of not knowing what happened to my friends flooded my already overflowing mind. If
~~~

they had turned to the side black of the chessboard then they must be under Pandora's control somewhere in this fortress of nightmares. The place was still pulsing like a beating heart and the vibration hit a nerve every time its magic thumped. The thing I hated most about this place was that it was alive and that crime against gods could see every little thing I was doing.

After what seemed like hours of wandering, I stopped hovering down the empty halls and took a breather on the floor. I was getting absolutely nowhere. There was no voice or Therion to guide me to where to go next. Just then I felt movement in my clothes. I had completely forgotten about chip in my pocket. I opened my shredded robe pocket and revealed the small bird to my tired eyes. He rolled around to face me, but something wasn't right. That usual chippy animal spirit had left his tiny atmosphere. I tried tickling him to cheer him up but he only snapped at my finger.

"Come on buddy, keep smiling for me." I bubbled. But he merely rolled around again into the comfort of my pocket. "At least I still have you, even if you're in a huff."

"Is that all you need your friends for? To cheer you up?" A voice came from the darkness.

I quickly floated to my feet and braced myself. "Pandora, enough of your games and let's settle this." I called out.

"Oh Raven. Don't you recognize the sweet sound of your friend's voice?" The voice was familiar and I knew it well.

I looked into the nothingness and could see the faint image of a body coming closer to me. I braced my magic for whatever could come at me and watched as the person came closer. They came out of the darkness and I was horrified to see who it was.

"Hey bestie." Layla chirped creepily.

But it wasn't the Layla I knew to be a cheerful and upbeat girl. Her eyes were black like tar, just like the gods. Her cheeks lost the bright pink glow and the sparkle in her smile faded like the sun outside the palace.

"Layla...not you." I whelped.

"What's wrong? Are you afraid of losing me too, as well as Jack?" Her voice echoed and deepened wickedly. She stared at me with her black depraved eyes and smiled as if there was nothing wrong with the current situation.

"What has she done to you?" I worried, trying to steer away from her gaze.

"Pandora only helped me." She creeped closer to

me as I shuffled on the floor away from her. "I have overcome the trauma you have caused me by taking me away from my home and the only world I loved with all my heart."

"No! You and Jack wanted to come!" I cried.

"You were leaving...what choice did we have? You put us in danger and here is where we have all ended up..." She needled at me

I knew this wasn't the real Layla I was talking to, but did she really think all of this? Was she forced to tell the truth by Pandora, or was it a web of lies? I floated to my feet and crept away from the creepy girl standing in front of me. But as I levitated backwards, I was stopped by something else. I turned around and was brought face to face with another set of scary black eyes. It was Jack, and he looked just as lifeless as Layla.

"Trying to give up on me again Ray? Abandoning me again? You forgot about me when *I* went missing, you never cared about me." His voice boomed in my ears.

"Jack, I would never abandon you-"

"Then why did you? Why did you only care about finding your father and the other gods? I was the last thing you thought about until you saw me at the palace entrance."

The guilt was making me fear the evil inside him even more. Did he speak the truth? Did I really ignore the fact he had gone missing and overlook an indispensable friend? No. Pandora was trying to fill my head with lies.

I looked dead straight into Jack's eyes. "At least I know that wasn't the real Jack giving me the cold shoulder."

His face made no expression of it, but I knew he was mad as he and Layla retreated back into the dark. I watched as they disappeared and took a sigh of relief. I lifted my feet from the ground, and floated down the halls once again, hoping that I wouldn't encounter anything worse than what I had just witnessed. But as I floated down, I felt like I was getting farther and farther away from danger, and I couldn't tell whether I was happy about it or not. Did I want to get closer, or as far away as my battered body could?

I was tired and weak after a long aimless wander, but I had to keep going, even if I had no idea where I was going. Then suddenly I saw something straight for me. It was big and it was coming fast! I casted a shield in front of me to protect myself, but I soon realized that wouldn't be necessary. It was a horse. It was a rich dark brown with a mane that flowed like a blonde waterfall. It stared right at me as the confusion dwindled in my eyes for a moment, then disappeared once I saw a head pop up from behind the horse's.

"Raven!" None other than Ophilia...on the horse.

"Ophilia!" I burst. She jumped down from the horse and jumped into my arms. The feeling to have someone in my presence after all this time was beyond soothing, this place tends to make one go insane.

"Thank Zeus I found you. This place is a labyrinth of lies!" She shuddered.

"Speaking of, how did you find me?" I asked. How was anyone meant to navigate this place?

"Actually, we didn't find you on purpose. We had a nasty run-in with Layla and Jack. After that we ran."

"Speaking of...again...where did you find that horse?"

"Maybe you should see you for yourself."

"What do you mean?"

"Look at him. Who do you see?" She hinted.

I floated over to the golden maned stead and looked at it. For a horse, he looked oddly familiar. I saw the courageous and determined spirit in his eyes, and that was when I knew who it was.

"Looking great Alfyn." I told him.

He nodded and I smiled at his accomplishment.

"Looks like you finally unlocked your power. I told you, you would eventually." I said and placed my hand on his face feeling the warmth in my palm.

"We had that nasty encounter with Layla and Jack." Ophilia said. "They attacked us from the dark and we tried our best to fight back, but Pandora's grip on them must have made them stronger. Just when they were about to finish the job, Alfyn's eyes started glowing bright orange. He started to change, and then suddenly he was the horse you see now. I jumped on his back he legged it."

I always knew he was destined for greatness. His passion to protect the people he cares about was the key to unlocking his true potential. At least now we can get around quicker. Ophilia and I mounted the back of Alfyn and we dashed down the dark hallway once again, his hooves clicking all the way.

"What happened when you guys disappeared?" I asked as I held onto Alfyn's mane with Ophilia's arms around my waist.

"I don't remember much to be honest. Last thing I recall was all of us standing in the room with all the gods and Pandora. Then I suddenly blacked out. I woke alone and without my staff, so I couldn't use my magic. Then after a bit of aimless walking, me and Alfyn found each other and here we are." She finished.

"Pandora tried to split us up, make us feel weak. Clever. She already got to Layla and Jack, but did you see Therion or Serenity?" I asked worriedly. I turned around and Ophilia shook her head.

If Ophilia and Alfyn got attacked, then the same could have happened to Serenity and Alfyn or worse, been corrupted by Pandora. I didn't want to do anything else until I knew they were both safe. I knew they were both strong, and I hated to admit it, but Pandora was stronger. That isn't real strength though. She feeds off the power of others and that proves she's weak on the inside. Real power comes from the inside. I didn't know yet how exactly we were meant to take her down, but everyone has a weakness, and hers might be the fact that she relies so much on the magic she has drained from the gods. If only we could release that power and give it back to who it belongs to.

We slowed Alfyn down and he came to a slow trot, we were dawdling at this point, not knowing where to. These halls were endless and I was getting tired of it.

"How long has it been since we've seen the sun?" Ophilia moaned. "And my arse is killing me. No offence Alfyn but your back isn't very comfortable."

He neighed in annoyance and kicked his hind legs, making Ophilia fall backwards.

"Thanks for that." She grunted and just laid back on Alfyn. "If only Therion were here so he could read minds and tell if we were getting close."

"Therion?" I asked.

"Yes? Therion, white hair, silver eyes, tends to read minds from time to time..." She mocked

"No look!" Therion." I yelled as I looked ahead of us and saw him on the floor. "Alfyn hurry up." I patted him and he sprinted towards Therion.

We reached him and we hopped off Alfyn. I knelt down to see if he was alright because he didn't look it. He was on his knees and his hands were gripping his bandaged forehead as if he was in pain.

"Therion? What's wrong? Are you okay?" His breathing was rapid and his eyes were swirling strongly.

"It's......Pandora......she's trying to.......get in my head." He shrieked.

"He must be trying to fight back." Ophilia suggested. "Don't let her, Therion! Keep fighting." She urged.

He yelled in agonizing pain. I couldn't imagine what kind of battle he was having in his head, Pandora fighting for control and Therion trying his hardest to defend his mind from her evil grip.

"Come on Therion, she may be strong, but your mind is far stronger than anyone's!"

Chip peaked his head from my pocket and chirped at Therion. He looked over at the bird in my pocket and smiled through the pain. Therion's head throbbing began to subside and his breathing calmed down.

"I believe......I believe the worst is over. My, that was awful." He sighed and relaxed on the floor to catch his breath.

"What happened in there?" I asked as I helped him to calm down.

His face looked frightened and the swirl in his eyes stopped, as if his magic had stopped temporarily. "She tried to corrupt my mind; she wants me under her control so she can know what others are thinking. It was excruciating. It was like a million knives trying to penetrate my mind while Pandora attempted to fill it with darkness and lies. She's envious of my unique magic and she wants it for herself, but I don't understand how I was able to keep her at bay."

"Maybe she gave up?" Ophilia suggested.

"No, she wouldn't have after trying so hard.

Something interfered with her grip on me, like someone cut the strings before they were intertwined."

"Well, whatever it is, thank you." I praised.

"One question." Therion added. "The horse...." He said looking up at Alfyn that loomed over him.

"Long story." I groaned and pulled him up from the ground.

Therion stopped in front of Alfyn and stared at him. "Hello Alfyn. You're a horse..."

Alfyn neighed and rubbed Therion's face with his.

"Therion. Were you able to figure out anything about Pandora while she was in your head?" I asked him.

"Yes. And in fact, I know how we can defeat her. I'll tell you as we keep going."

We mounted on Alfyn again and Therion told us how we could take Pandora down once and for all.

"She has a box; it's supposedly meant to be 'Pandora's box' of legend. They say whenever she opened it, calamity would rain down in the place it was opened. "

"So, we have to destroy the box?" Ophilia suggested?

"No, it can't be destroyed. She has flipped the system and instead of filling it with chaos and destruction, she has filled it with the power of our gods." He corrected.

"So, if we open the box..." I started.

"The gods get their magic back!" Ophilia finished.

"Exactly. It's like a bubble waiting to burst. All we have to do is pop said bubble." Therion said.

Very clever. I was confused up until now how anyone could handle that much power directly, but she has it in her box and that's how she's staying alive. She may be a god but not even she would be able to possess that much magic at once. Very clever indeed.

"So where is this box?" Ophilia asked.

"I can tell you that...," said a random voice.

Alfyn stopped dead in his tracks and we all fell forward slightly. He started neighing aggressively and we looked up to see what was wrong.

"Alfyn what's wrong? And who said that?"

I looked into the darkness and tried to see what Alfyn was seeing, then I saw another person coming from it. They came closer and the excitement flooded my heart when I saw who it was.

“Serenity!” I cheered. I jumped off Alfyn and ran over to her, but I stopped when I didn’t see her sparkling emerald eyes and only saw the void where they were meant to be.

“No... not you too.” I whimpered. I couldn’t cope with the fact I had lost her to the darkness. First Jack, then Layla and now Serenity. I didn’t know how much more this torture I could take. The warm red glow from her cheeks had disappeared and her golden blonde hair had lost its glimmer. That wasn’t the girl I loved.

“Oh Raven.” She sighed pitifully and placed her cold hand on my face. She looked at me but I just looked away, not wanting to have to stare into her lifeless eyes. “You always knew I would break your heart one way or another.”

“Don't do this.” I begged and removed her hand from my face but held it firmly. “We love each other and I'm ready to admit that. We both have a passion for our realms and fighting for who we love. And I'm ready to fight for you. Fight Pandora’s grip and realize it.”

“I never loved you. I never felt a single thing for you...no one ever will.” She stabbed with an emotionless grin.

A dagger had just struck me with the words I’d never thought would escape such a person's mouth.

"Nothing hurts more than a blow to the heart. You spent all this time getting here to see your father again. But this is where it ends. Thanks to you, we're trapped here forever. I won't be able to feel the warmth of my mother's smile ever again."

"No." I snapped and overcame my shattered heart. None of this is real, and I know that now. My aunt is trying to distract me from what I need to do, but it doesn't matter to me anymore.

"This isn't Serenity saying these cursed things." I wasn't with her anymore; I was talking through her. "Serenity is kind, Serenity is thoughtful, and she is far from this puppet you have turned her into, Pandora! So, go ahead, try and fill my head with lies because I have stopped believing them. You know how to play the game, I'll give you that, but the nightmare ends now." I protested and looked deep into Serenity's black eyes knowing Pandora was listening.

The silence was shattering as I waited bravely for a response.

"Fine. You can have your girlfriend back." Pandora's voice said from Serenity's mouth. The black in her eyes snapped away and the color in her skin returned. She collapsed from being weak and I caught her in my arms. The strings had been cut. I looked at her and saw the beautiful girl that I missed.

Her eyes opened and focused on mine. "Raven..."

"I'm here." I told her and smiled. I hugged her tightly and felt happy to be with her again. I didn't know what I had until it was gone. I'm never going to take her for granted again.

"It was awful. She forced me to say those things and.......I'm sorry." She pleaded to me.

I knew that those words weren't hers and it was something she couldn't control.

"Don't you dare apologize. That wasn't you. I know you didn't mean it. But I meant every word *I* said." I proclaimed.
"I know." She swooned. "You can tell me again when this is all over."

She leaned up and kissed my cheek. My cheeks lit hot, and I felt my face turn bright red and she giggled. I looked over at the others and they were trying their hardest to act as natural as possible. Alfyn neighed in excitement and trotted his hooves.

"Isn't that just precious. Makes me sick!" Pandora's voice snapped and echoed from the darkness.

The blackness around us faded and things started to seem real, but I immediately wished it back. We were back in the room with all the gods and Pandora.

"Welcome back." She sarcastically cheered. "I hope you enjoyed my little hall of fun."

22

ONE LAST LOOK

~~~

We all stood up and faced the table of gods in front of us, still looking as lifeless and creepy. The chessboard still in the middle of the table, but this time all my friend's pieces turned to the white side standing beside me. We knew how to stop all this though, and the box was floating right beside Pandora. It was small but decorated nicely. It was brown with gold plated on its corners and had gems that glowed purple. Magenta particles fizzed from it, and you could tell it was holding a lot of power inside. I didn't really have a plan to open it while it was that close to Pandora, but I knew I would figure something out. Alfyn transformed back into his normal self so we could all stand together as our true selves.

"So, the knight became its own stead?" Pandora mocked.

"That's one way of putting it bluntly." He defended.

I had my eyes on the box the entire time, trying to
~~~

think of way to open the stupid thing. Therion must have read my mind because he looked at me right after I thought of it.

"You must have figured it out by now, Therion." My aunt called down the table.

"That opening the box is the solution to your demise? Yes, I have."

"Well then you know the consequences of it."

Him and I looked at each other not knowing what she was talking about. It should be as easy as opening a box...which is exactly what we need to do.

"What kind of consequences?" I pondered.

"For the love of Zeus.......My box contains the power of every god in the universe. Combined, that power could re-fabricate an entire world. If a person were to take that power upon them directly, the consequences would be fatal. In short, open the box, you die. Get the picture?" She scowled.

"But If we don't...trillions of people will suffer beneath your foot." I realized.

"Indeed. So since you're out of moves…I believe that is checkmate, my dear nephew." She cackled and her black piece directly moved a space in-front of mine, securing her victory.

Her laugh sent chills through my spine and my neck hairs stood even thinner. She had thought of this every way possible, thinking of every loophole in the book. I looked at my father and thought of the disappointment I must have caused him. Medusa beside him was making me feel uneasy and all their lifeless eyes looking straight ahead without emotion.

"Everyone." Therion announced quietly and our heads turned to him. "I know what must be done."

"Please tell me you have an idea because my hope for defeating this demon is slowly dying." Ophilia prayed.

Therion looked at it with uncertainty but also determination. I knew he had an idea but he himself wasn't happy with it.

"Raven." He said and came to me. "It has been an absolute honor, watching out and serving you."

I was puzzled. "Therion what are you-"

He put his hand on my shoulder and a tear rolled down his face. "Please tell your father I said thank you. Thank you for giving me a reason to keep going." He said and turned to the table.

"Wait what hold on-" I realized what he was about to do. "NO WAIT THERION!"

He dashed down the room and jumped onto the

table. I called out his name, begging him to come back but Serenity had held me close. He ran down the table towards the puppet master. He looked back at my father and gave a proud look to him. Therion leaped into the air to grab the box, but his fate was rewritten when Layla and Jack appeared and struck him with their blade's midair.

"NOOO!" I cried.

He fell to the floor from the air as his blood splattered and leaked into the tiles. His shredded body had fallen facing me and his eyes looked at me as he held onto his last bit of life. But Jack wasn't finished. He walked over to Therion menacingly as he faded away on the floor. Jack gripped his sword thrusted the blade through Therion's chest, not even batting an eye. I fell to my knees in grief, tears pouring down my face and drenching the floor beneath me. I looked up to see Jack standing over him holding his sword now saturated in Therion's blood. Pandora reached over to the chessboard and flicked his piece of the table and smashed when it hit the floor.

"What a fool." She chuckled. "Did he really think that was going to work?"

The sadness and rage spun around my mind as I watched Pandora laugh at my friend's demise, his lifeless body lying there. He was loyal to the very end. Served my father with pride. Protected me and my people without hesitation. And just like that, when he was only trying to do the right thing, for the sake of others.

“Now as I was saying.” Pandora sighed as if nothing happened. “Is this you finally coming to terms of surrender?”

Being blinded by grief and rage, I flew to my feet and glided down the room just like Therion did before me. I jumped on the table dashing towards the box. My friends were screaming and shouting at me, but I couldn’t let the suffering go on, it had to end here and now. Jack and Layla tried to stop me, but I propelled them away with my magic and launched myself towards the box. Time seemed to slow down as I saw Pandora with that panicky look on her face and my friends calls in my mind.

“I'm sorry everyone.” I thought.

This is how it ends. This is the universe I have suffered in. Felt happy in. Safe in. And even fallen in love in. Bad things always happen to wrong people, and something not even I can change. But what it's worth, before I drift off and join my mother and Therion. May the stars in every sky, in every realm, shine a little brighter now that I will become a part of them.

I grabbed the box and flicked the lid open. An unfathomably bright shock wave shot out of the box and knocked everyone in the room backwards, but I held on. The magic of the most powerful beings in all existence flooded out of the box and passed through me. The pain being worse than all the pain I have ever felt combined. I screamed in deathly agony as I tried to keep the box open long enough, but I couldn't hold on much longer. My sight started to become hazy as I started to slip away, and drifted into the light...

....

I saw nothing but bright white, not knowing where I was. Am I dead? Is this the afterlife? But then the light began to form, and things started to become clear. I saw something directly in front of me and when it all became clear, I was confused to see it was Chip. He chirped at me as I started to wake up and regain my consciousness. His white feathered face and shiny pearl eyes were right on my face and I giggled at his persistence. I sat up and he fluttered into my hands. But then I looked around and realized where I was. I didn't know why, but I was back in Charissa's library. It was warm and cozy like it once was, and the feeling of relaxation reminded me of the first time I walked in.

Chip flew out of my hands and fluttered down the library and behind the door that led to the room that Charissa took me into when we first met. I got to my feet and followed Chip into the room and opened the door to see where he flew off to, but I was taken by surprise when I was welcome by a surprising and familiar face, Charissa.

“Hello again dear.” She beamed as she sat there discretely sipping her tea.

Bewildered doesn’t come close to what I was feeling, but soon came to the conclusion that the blast from the box had killed me and I was dead. This illusion of Charissa’s library being Heaven itself because it's a place I felt safe in.

“It’s nice to see you again Charissa. But why am I here?” I asked, still astonished to be where I was. Emotions weren't really overcoming me at this point because I still believed I was dreaming.

“Sit darling and will be explained. "She suggested and pointed to the cushion in front of her, sipping a hot beverage from her cup. The déjà vu was unreal.

I sat in front of her and examined her face, and she definitely was the woman I remembered.

“Why am I here and not in the afterlife?”

“You're not dead *yet* my dear.” She chuckled.

“Then why am I here?”

“Because I believe you deserve a second chance. I have been with you this entire time and watched you overcome so many obstacles, and I think we can both agree you don't deserve to give up the amazing family you have found for yourself." She explained.

"What do you mean you have been with me this entire time? What happened to you? Why did you disappear?" I questioned.

"Easy my dear boy." She settled. You see Raven, I am Chip." She said and sipped her drink.

At this point I knew I was dead. That was the most ridiculous thing I had ever heard. How could a human woman be a bird?

I laughed but she didn't seem amused. "You're not kidding?"

"No, I'm afraid I'm not." She scoffed. "And not only am I Chip, but I am also your grandmother. I'm Rhea's mother."

Now I was beyond confused.

"Let me explain." She started. "Your mother and your aunt are my children, but Pandora already told you about the biggest regret of my life. I jumped to conclusions too quickly and put my own daughter's life in the hands of fate, without letting her write her own story. Rhea never told you about me or your aunt because she feared that you would be connected to the prophecy and didn't want you in any part of it."

"Fortuna only showed what could happen, and I poorly believed every bit of it, and by casting her away and imprisoning her, only confirmed my worst fears. Over the years I became weak from constantly having to channel my magic into containing Pandora. Then when she broke out, she overthrew me, robbed me of me, of my godly powers, trapped and banished me to earth with no way to return to Althea. Rhea had no knowledge of my disappearance, but soon did after Pandora sent that snake after her and corrupted her pure heart. When you walked into my library on that day, I immediately saw my daughter's eyes in yours and knew you were my grandson."

"I didn't want to overwhelm you while your mind was still fragile, so I didn't tell you that I was your grandmother. But when you told me that you had lost your mother and your family, my heart shattered. You didn't see it at the time, but I didn't have much longer after that. So, I gave you the key to Therion's old house to help you as best I could. Then my body gave up on me, and I disappeared into the cosmos."

"However, I refused to leave it. You see when a god passes away, their body turns into a bright glowing dust so it can become one with the stars. My soul longed for a better ending than that. So, by using what little strength I had left in my spirit, I took the form of the small white bird that you decided to name Chip, so I could protect and watch over you. Soon after my reincarnation, I realized that since I was the Goddess of Protection, my gift to protect anyone I was near, passed on even after death.

"That's why Pandora couldn't reach me." I realized. "It's why her corruptive magic could touch me."

"Yes. And since you overcame the grief of your mother's loss and risked your life many times to save the universe, I am giving you the second chance you deserve." She praised.

"A second chance?" I wondered bright eyed and looked at her intently.

"Since the spirits gave me a second chance, I am going to pass that onto you so you can live again..."

My heart filled with gratitude, but then wondered...." What will happen to you?"

"Don't you mean what will happen to Chip?" She chuckled. "I'm afraid Chip and I won't be with you when you return. But I will still watch over my grandson, this time from the stars."

The thought of not having Chip in my pocket anymore hurt to think about. But if it meant I could be with my father and my amazing friends again, then it's a sad thought I am willing to live with. Greif is an old friend. I would never forget

Charissa's kindness and that her memory would live on with me forever. I got up from the cushion and knelt down before her, wrapping my arms around her, showing my gratitude and love to my grandmother.

"Thank you. Not just for now, but everything." I professed.

She hugged me back and held me tightly with her gentle arms and radiating warmth. "Tell her I'm sorry...Pandora. Tell me if I could take it all back I would." She whispered in my ear.

"I don't think she will understand that easily, but I will." I said and pulled away.

She smiled and looked at me with the twinkle in her eye I saw when we first met. This woman will never be forgotten.

"Would you care for a drop of tea before you go?" She offered.

"Thanks, but no." I giggled.

"Well in that case-" she said and put her cup down and placed her hands on her chest. "This is goodbye."

"Goodbye Charissa."

She closed her eyes and her body started to shine bright like the sun. Her body began to disintegrate to magical golden dust. Her dust formed itself into a bright glowing ball of light and it floated towards me. I reached out and touched it, and everything became white once again.

Hearing faint sounds, my vision blurry once again, but everything coming together like it always does. Serenity's face came clear to me as she held me in her arms sobbing.

"What's going on?" I grunted and tried to sit up.

Serenity's face froze when she looked up and saw that life had returned to my body.

"You're alive!" She cried and jumped into my weak arms knocking us both to the floor. She broke away from the hug and pressed her lips against mine. My heart instantly went a million miles per hour as we shared our first kiss. Her face was wet and warm from crying after thinking I was dead. But when I saw the face I wanted to see for ten years appear behind Serenity, I began to cry myself. My father, no longer corrupted by darkness and the light returned to his eyes. I jumped to my feet, slightly wobbling from my broken leg, and jumped into his big arms.

"My son, my boy." He whimpered manly, but I didn't care what anyone thought at this point> I had finally reunited with my father and no one was going to ruin this for me. I felt his large wings wrapping around us bringing us close, feeling his heartbeat against my ear. My hair slightly getting wet from his tears as they landed on my head. He pulled away, knelt down and held my shoulders firmly in front of him to see all of me.

He was lost for words, but who could blame him?

"Raven, I am so proud of you... and I'm sorry I didn't find you sooner..." He whelped and lowered his head.

I lifted his head by his horns and brought him face to face. "There's no need to apologize, we're together now, and I'm not going anywhere." I told him and hugged him again.

I looked behind my father as I hugged and saw the supporting looks the rest of the reformed gods were giving me, thumbs up and salutes. The god I recognized as Hermes picked up the chessboard that laid on the table, hurled it at the wall and smashed it. The entire palace had got its color and light back to. There was no more darkness and there were actually windows that led to the outside world. Serenity ran over to her mother and they did the same thing my father and I were doing.

Fertility looked a lot like her realm. She wore a long green moss cape covered in bloomed flowers and a gown made from white rose petals that glimmered silver in the light that now filled the room.

Ophilia, Alfyn, Layla and Jack pounced on me out of nowhere and began smothering the life out of me with hugs. Layla and Jack were now back to their true selves, but I don't think they realized what they had done. But then that reminded me. I broke away from the group hug and walked over to the brave soul we had lost. Therion's lay cold and motionless. I gently placed my fingers over his eyes and closed them, then removed my shredded robe and respectively placed it over him until we could bury him where he belonged. Everyone gathered around, my father placing a hand on my shoulder. But then we all heard a loud grunting in the corner of the room, that had ruined the moment.

Pandora pulled herself up from behind the table, looking weak and very powerless. The whole creepy puppet master physique had faded away along with her magic. She looked at me and her face grew red with rage.

"You....You just had to go and ruin everything didn't you? I gave you the option to join me but Noooo, you had to go and be a hero to save everyone" She rambled.

Everyone God in the room shared a look and we all knew what had to be done. We all clicked our fingers and a large magic bubble popped around my malicious aunt, incarcerating her for the time being. We all laughed as she struggled and rolled around in the bubble. I know she suffered in the past and that's why she did all this, but it's what she deserved until we figured out what to do with her.

But while everyone else laughed and cheered that they were finally free from Pandora's control, I couldn't help but feel like something was missing. That's when I heard a faint call coming from the other side of the room, where Medusa was sitting. I limped over to see what it was, but it wasn't Medusa....It was my mother.

My mind didn't give a thought to dash over and help her. I held her in my arms and faced her towards me, seeing her beautiful and kind face for the first time in ten years. But she was weak and could barely focus me before her, but when she realized who was holding her, her face slowly lit up.

"Raven?" She said weakly, her voice shaken and shriveled.

"I'm here mother." My voice slightly cracked with overwhelming joy inside me. I hadn't laid eyes on this woman in over a century. The woman that brought me joy and happiness in my childhood. Although I was afraid to say it, I felt her slipping away again.

She reached up and gently held my face, and I felt the cold of her hand. I held it as I looked at her, her red eyes slowly losing the life that once filled them.

"She doesn't have long." My father said and knelt

down beside me." Pandora revived her and kept her alive. Now that she's been defeated, your mother will return to the place she was revived from."

"Your father....is right. But listen my sweet child......I'm so proud...You will be.... a great king...when the time comes."

She struggled and smiled once last time before her last breath. Her body glowed and shined, I held onto her tight, not wanting to let go. Rhea faded into the magical glowing dust and I looked at my hands, wishing she was still in them. Hermes opened the large window that stood behind the table, for the dust to rise and drift away upon the skies of Althea, her own realm. I watched as my mother rose into the sky and dwindled into the stars themselves, becoming one with her realm. My father held me firmly as everyone in the room paid their respects to the great queen that brought me into this beautiful but chaotic universe...

23

GONE BUT NOT FORGOTTEN

~~~

With all of us returned to Atlasdam, we had to perform one final act before we could return to normal. We brought Therion back from Althea, and silently decided he deserved to be remembered for years to come. He served his people and friends righteously and without hesitation. The loyalty that was Therion should never be forgotten. My father had a very special resting place built for him, in the mountains behind the city. Serenity and her mother Fertility used their magic to decorate it beautifully with gorgeous and unique fauna.

We spread the word of Therion's death and many people from several realms turned up to pay their respects. Even Hastings came out of his way to give a snarky remark and gloated how 'close' he was with him, though not many paid much attention. Apparently, Darius and Therion had history together as well because he got up in front of everyone and regaled us with old times they had. He was loved and appreciated by many, and I didn't think for a second why. He was an extraordinary
~~~

and outgoing man, and even though he wasn't a god, he sure of hell acted like one. He looked out for the people he cared about and was always honored to earn the respect of others. My father chose him because he knew he would give it his all to his cause, and always stay loyal to the people that treat him right.

After we held a funeral for him, I stayed back at his grave to pay my final respects and thank him for everything he had done for me, my father, and our people. Ophilia and Alfyn snuck up on me by accident and I nearly blasted them through the roof.

"How you holding up bud?" Alfyn asked kindly and put his arm around me, a bit of sadness in his voice.

"I'm doing fine, but what about Layla and Jack? They must be beating themselves up." I wondered and looked back to see where they were. When I told them and Pandora made them do this, they didn't take it very well. They both knew it wasn't their fault, but I would feel horrendous if I was forced against my fill to take my will to take my friends life.

"I spoke to them earlier." Ophila said. "They knew that it wasn't their fault, but they're still upset that it happened by their own hands."

"Do you think Therion would have understood?"

"Definitely." They spoke.

"How are you feeling about your mother and all?" Ophilia asked, trying to sound as supportive as possible.

"I felt that empty feeling ten years ago, the second I realized that it wasn't my mother I was seeing. So, in a way, her leaving isn't something I'm new to, you know?" I admitted.

They both hugged me, our thick winter coats stopping us from going all the way. We laughed at this and walked out of the memorial, feeling the cold mountain air tickle our noses. There was Pegasus waiting for Ophilia, to bring her back down to the city. She mounted the horse and Alfyn transformed into one himself and flew off while I took one last look at Therion's grave.

"Till we meet again. Say hello to my mother and grandmother, will you?" I said to myself and leaped off the ground to the skies following Alfyn and Ophilia.

When I got back from the mountain, I looked for my father in the palace, and found him in a hallway. He was gazing at one of the family portraits we had painted when I was only a child. My parents were cradling me in their arms, both happy that I had come into the world. My father's beard was short and his horns weren't as long as they were now.

One of his wings was folded on his back, while the other was around my mother.

"She always lectured me about them, my wings." My father chimed after the long deafening silence of gazing at the painting. "She used to say, "Watch where you're flapping those before you blow someone away." He chuckled.

"Was this before or after I was born?" I asked, trying to make small talk.

"Before. She never wanted to bicker in front of you, thinking it would have a bad influence."

There was another long silence, I didn't know what to say anymore.

"We spoke a lot while we were trapped in our own minds. It was like all of us were in a prison in our heads, and we could speak to each other. Rhea and I only worried about what had come of you. Were you alive? Were you dead? You were the only thing we thought about while we were trapped for those months."

"It must have been horrible. Not being able to control your own body and watching as your power is used to cause suffering." I tried to comfort but I didn't know if it was working or not.

"Ha, it was. But oddly enough, believe it or not, we were at peace with ourselves. We admitted to ourselves that was it, that we would be trapped forever, thinking no one could overpower Pandora, until you came along and saved us all."

Thinking back at it now, I never did think that I would be able to pull it off. I may have pulled off some surprising stunts, like escaping the underworld or taking on the Leviathan. But facing the combined power of the gods was nothing I could ever imagine doing.

"It wasn't just me. I had my friends beside me to keep pushing me, I couldn't have done it without them." I told my father. "Ophilia and Alfyn didn't want to give up until they saw you safe back here."

"What about your human friends? I believe they were quite the credit to your return here."

"Yeah, they're great. Both of them have been with me since I crashed on earth. They understood my pain and loss, and were always curious to learn about the world of magic. Is it alright if they stay here? I don't think they want to go back." I asked, but something about my father's facial expression told he wasn't on board.

He turned and looked down at me. "You know better than anyone that I created this realm to be a safe haven for people who want to start anew. But when it comes to your human friends that have no knowledge of our ways and laws, could greatly impact their development as people. Are you sure that's what they really want?"

"Yes, it is your highness." Someone called out.

I turned around and saw Layla and Jack standing behind me, both with confused faces.

"I know we don't have magic like you guys, and we may not know how things work here. But we're both willing to learn all we need to know." Layla claimed.

She smiled and me then elbowed Jack. He looked up and forced a smile on himself.

"Of course, yeah, willing to learn...." He said and looked at my father, looking slightly intimidated. "Sorry. I'm still a bit shaken up about the whole...thing." He sighed

"Don't worry son. We're all still trying to get over the traumatic events that took place, but we will be alright." My father supported.

"Thanks Triton, I mean-" Jack went into a professional stance. "Thank you, sir!"

I laughed to myself but kept it in, my father doing the same.

"Well then, consider yourselves the newest citizens of Atlasdam." Triton commended. "You're welcome to stay here in the palace or you could have your very own home in the city."

"I think they're better off staying here." I butted in. "Let them get a bit more familiar with the place before they have their own place." I grinned, thinking that would be the best choice.

"Yes, that sounds lovely, thank you." Layla said.

"Yeah, really appreciate it." Jack added.

A maid came down the hall and my father asked her to show them the pair to their new rooms. They went down the hall excited with the maid, confused what was going on.

"Good kids." My father approved. "But for some reason I can't help but think I have met them before.

"Probably just you imagining things father." I chuckled and walked away giggling.

"What about Fertility's girl? What's she like?" He called after me."

"Amazing! About to see her now!" I said and opened the window next to me.

I gave my father one last smile and jumped out feeling the wind in my face as gravity dragged me through the sky. Before I plummeted into the ground, I used my magic to land safely on my two feet. I landed in the courtyard and saw Alfyn and

Ophilia talking to Hasting's and Darius. Hastings was holding the weapon that he made for Alfyn and he looked like he was showing Darius. I hesitated to go over and join them, but the looks Ophilia was giving me were practically begging me to help her get out of there.

"Hey Ophilia, can you come here for a sec?" I called her, pretending it was important.

She looked relieved to finally step away from Hastings. "From the bottom of my heart, thank you. I was this close to launching him all the way back to Coldera." She bantered looking fed up.

"He's not that bad." I lied to myself "After all, if it wasn't for him, we wouldn't have found my father and everyone else."

"He won't stop going on about that! How if it wasn't for him the 'universe would have ended.'"

I glanced over at him and he was cackling like a vulture. "Yeah, I can see how that could get irritating. Have you seen Serenity by the way?"

"Turn around." She pointed behind me.

I spun around and saw Serenity going into the gardens. "Thanks, I'll see you later...and good luck."

"Don't leave me!" Ophilia called out as I ran after Serenity.

The gardens were always a great comfort after a long day. The calming atmosphere and the surrounding fauna couldn't help but make you feel relaxed. Fertility grew even more flowers as a way of saying thank you for saving her, so it was even more beautiful than before. She grew many unique flowers, all with their own special properties, but my favorite was a crystalized tree she planted beside me and my mother's statue. It was like a normal tree, but every part of it was made of a different crystal. The leaves were bright green emeralds and the bark was made of a rich dark brown Citrine gemstone. It was shiny and transparent, and when the sun came down on it, it glimmered like a thousand stars, casting sparkly rainbows upon the rest of the garden. I gazed through it and noticed something on the other side but couldn't make out what it was. But the girl I had been thinking about all day popped out from behind it.

"You're welcome for all this." She jokingly boasted. "I did help my mother out with planting all this, especially this here tree. She needs a lot of strength to pull this one from the ground."

"Is she around? I really want to thank her directly."

"No, she's helping locking Pandora in the darkest pits of Tartarus."

"You mean the godly prison that takes up the space of an entire realm?"

"Yep, that's the one. It's where she belongs for all the pain and suffering she caused." Serenity spat spitefully.

"I know but she had suffered a lot too. Then again, I agree, that's not an excuse to take it out on others. A lot of people will be out for her so Tartarus is really the best place for her." I said trying to make things light.

"We don't have to think about it anymore. It's all over." She said and sat me down with her by the fountain. "By the way, I think you have something to say to me young man." She played.

"Oh, would you care to remind me?" I played back.

She pulled me closer, and we gazed at each other's eyes before we pressed our lips together once more. I pulled her close to me and felt the warmth of her body against mine. No one was going to ruin this moment while we kissed by the fountain in the middle of the place of my childhood.

I broke away and looked into her eyes. "I love you. Happy now?"

She pushed me backwards and I fell right into the water, her diving right on top of me. We splashed around and laughed like quite the pair. It was weird to think that if none of this happened, we would have never met. Everyone saw Pandora as the villain of the story, but in the end, she was the one that brought us all together.

A NOTE FROM THE AUTHOR

Greeting to the amazing person that chose to read this book. I just wanted to say how grateful I am you chose to place your trust in me to tell you a good story, and I do hope you enjoyed it.

I started out writing ridiculous stories when I was only a teenager and refused to show anyone what my imagination came up with. But when someone told me I should apply that creativity to something greater it gave me the motivation I needed to chase my dream to share my stories with others.

The fantasy of Raven has been in the making for the past four years (at the time of publishing) and I honestly can't believe I now get to share it with others. To achieve something so passionate at seventeen is beyond what I could put into words. But don't worry, the magic won't end here. Look out for future *Not One World* stories, because my imagination is far too big for just one book.

Printed in Great Britain
by Amazon

70820732R00151